Haven's Helix

Book 1
Lost Hero

Eric Schneider

ISBN: 9781709153556 (Paperback)

This book is a work of fiction. Any references to historical events, real people, or real places are used fictitiously. Names, characters, and places are products of the author's imagination and any resemblance to actual events, places or persons, living or dead, is entirely coincidental.

Front cover image by Justin Schneider.

Printed in the United States of America.

First printing edition 2020

Haven's Helix
Book 1

Lost Hero

Eric Schneider

1

Control. A beautiful thing. Meaning to have power or influence over one's own actions. Something I wish I had.

The story begins in eastern Oregon. I was a young fifteen-year-old freshman who barely managed to get by. Nevertheless, I always ended up with quality grades, and a small group of friends. Sadly Though, I never could escape my own problems. I lived my entire fifteen years with high stress and low self-esteem. My entire life was spent in fear of every move I made, every word I said. I watched as my own mother went through hell only to support the two of us.

My father had mysteriously died before I could have a chance to remember him, leaving both of us to fend for ourselves. She tried her best to find love again, but never could. Every relationship always ended in anger and bitter tears. The latter from my mother's side.

This isn't even to mention the one variable that can never be predicted. Other people. I was almost always bullied from the moment I started school. Normally I could shake it off, the whole "what do they know" thing. Then there's that one fateful day.

Nothing had really been inherently different than any other day. I woke up at a normal time, left my home with enough time to get to school, and then proceeded to muddle with anxiety while suffering through midterms. It actually seemed pretty ironic how I would always score decently, but stress out for every second until I had heard my teacher telling us to put our pencils down. I wasn't even really scared of anything. In fact, I actually enjoyed the challenge of the many subjects. But in thinking about them, my mind immediately began to race to the nearest worst-case scenario and I would sometimes begin to panic. Nevertheless though, I was able to finish each one with as much effort as I needed to feel proud of myself, knowing that I would return the next day to see that I had passed each and every one of them. It was at that point when I packed up my things and began to head to the bus. The moment of my day which I had dreaded the most.

Even though I had lived less than maybe a half hour walk from school, I had chosen to ride the bus home each day. Even through the offers I had been given by friends were so enticing, I declined and continued to take the sometimes-hour-long ride home. The reason for this, I would always tell myself was for ease, but that wasn't even close to the case.

In my short walk to the other end of the school where the busses were kept and the students were corralled for their trip home, a small, insignificant question entered my mind.

"What am I doing to myself?" I quietly said without anyone noticing. "Every day I continue this constant torment. And for what? Sure, everything might seem fine on paper, but am I really happy? Am I content with myself? With all of this?"

Only a second later a small minute voice whispered in my thoughts. *'What is it that you want then? What do you truly want with your life?'*

The question seemed so abrupt, yet honest as if it had come from the deepest recesses of my desires. It was a question any teenager ponders at least once in their lives. But whenever I thought about it, it made me feel completely helpless, as if all the hope had been drained out from my body.

I shrugged off the voice, almost ignoring it. "This isn't the time or place," I said defiantly. "Everything's going to be fine soon. I just need to make it home. Then I'll be okay... then I can move along. Haah... Until tomorrow that is."

I continued walking at a brisk pace, avoiding what I had been asked. But I knew all too well what my answer was. What I truly wanted.

I wanted to be different. To be more than just the statue on a pedestal people had once placed me on. I wanted to be unique. To be special.

I wanted to live my life, just as I desired.

As I entered the bus, I was instantly pelted by the smell of intense perfume covering up other smells which would get other students expelled. Only if the bus driver actually cared at all to do something though. I frankly couldn't stand the odor but lacked the courage to walk up to the people I knew were smoking and tell them off, so I swallowed hard and trudged past the seats, through the aisle littered with backpacks and personal items until I finally reached an empty seat.

I laid back and finally took a breath of relief. Throughout all the work my stress could finally be gone and I would be able to enjoy the next couple days of school without any kind of stress of anxiety.

Within five minutes the bus had begun to move which began to lull me into a light trance. I began to zone out, staring at the scenery in front of me which I had seen every day. A part of me felt at peace and I began to wonder if I had been worrying about the bus ride for nothing.

"Well, isn't this certainly a paintable sight to see," I heard a voice say from beside me, knocking me completely out of my earlier trance. It was a voice I had been dreading to hear yet still knew was coming.

The voice was coming from another boy who would have only known me from the transport. His friends called him Shane, but I knew him as the one who had tortured me almost every day since the sixth grade. I didn't know at all what I could say to make him leave, but I knew I had to say something or else the situation would lead to something much worse than it could be. "Just leave me alone. I don't want to do this today."

Shane laughed and sat down right next to me, nearly pushing my body against the wall of the bus. "Hilarious," he said in a voice which made him seem friendly, but I knew it was only an act. "I'll tell you what, just because you have me in a good mood today, I might be able to lay off for a short while... for a small price of course."

He had pulled this stunt on me probably six times, giving me an ultimatum of paying him something around twenty bucks or enduring the same onslaught as I was used to, sometimes even harsher than normal. I had actually gone the route of paying him once or twice just to escape him for one day, but like every other time I lacked the funds and self-hatred to do so. I just stayed quiet, continuing to stare out the window.

Without looking at him, I knew Shane was becoming impatient with me, but I still held my ground and continued to look away. "Hello, did you not hear me this time. I'm clearly giving you an out and I suggest you take it." I continued to stare away from him.

After a few second Shane finally gave up on being nice, grabbing me by the shoulders of my shirt and fully pushing me against the wall of the bus. "Alright, so you're either deaf or crazy because only a complete idiot would ignore someone they know can make their day a living hell, but just because I am so generous, I'll give you one more chance. Twenty bucks, or your life."

In my mind I could picture his teeth becoming bared fangs and his voice snarling as he spoke.

Through my heart beating out of my chest, I managed to let out a couple fearful words. "Just get off of me will you. I don't have any money."

Shane narrowed his eyes, still holding me in place before suddenly releasing his grasp. I was free, but my heart was still beating louder than it had in days. He might have released me from his grip but he still wasn't about to just leave me be. "I guess that leaves the harder way then," he said while sighing loudly. "You know what your problem is. You don't realize where you belong in this world."

I kept silent, wishing that for once I had chosen to just walk home. But I knew that if I chose that route, Shane would just collect on the missing debt the next day at school. Either way, he continued to rant in an ominous tone. "You're just weak. You don't know when you're beaten or even outmatched, and you continue to piss me off. I bet you couldn't even fight back against me if you wanted to. After all, why in Hell's name would you want to make such a suicide attempt. You wouldn't even know the first thing of what you were doing." He paused, coming up with an idea. He leaned in close continuing his verbal assault. "In fact, why don't you just hit me right now, right here," he said pointing to the bottom of his chin. His voice became even more shrill and ominous than before. "Go ahead already. I dare you! Hit me!"

After the words left his mouth, I blacked out hearing nothing but my heart beating behind my chest. I couldn't see what I did next, and was at the mercy of whatever part of me took control.

*   *   *   *   *

I woke up in a police interrogation room hours later. My mind was so fragmented at this point that I couldn't even focus on the police officer screaming his head off at me.

"You do realize you could have killed people, and you tell me you don't care," I heard him say when my brain could understand the English language again. "I can overlook everything you've said to me if you answer my first question, why you attacked the bus and sent fifteen people to the hospital."

It took me a moment to realize what he had said. And even then, I couldn't comprehend what he was telling me. "Excuse me... what did you just say I did, my mind is a blur, I can hardly think."

The officer looked as if he was about to snarl. "What I just said is that you're in serious trouble. After all, there are some still unconscious as I speak because of you."

I didn't believe him. I couldn't believe him. In all my life I had never committed a violent act, so hearing that fifteen people were in the hospital due to an act I didn't even remember seemed utterly preposterous. "I'm sorry, but I find it hard to believe that's even possible," I said holding my hand to my head like a young adult with a hangover.

The officer scowled at me. "You can say all the excuses you want, we caught it all on tape," he said, pulling a VHS out of a desk drawer and placing it in the television mounted on the wall. In a normal case I would have laughed at how primitive the technology was, but both my haze and fear kept my mouth glued shut.

The video played, and immediately I recognized the bus I rode home on almost every day turning onto the street corner. As it did this though, a window broke and a student was thrown out the opening. I recognized him as Shane, the kid who was taunting me. The bus came to a sudden stop only a second after and another figure exited the bus through the emergency side door. He was a man who looked like me, but I didn't recognize him. There was just something that was different, and not just physically. This man had a black streak going through his right eye and down his cheek and arms, but more than that, his aura was completely different from mine. He was full of rage while I was normally content yet a little anxious.

Once the person exited the bus, he turned towards Shane laying on the ground unconscious. The man sneered in disgust and without hesitation, reentered the bus. At the angle I couldn't see very well, but I did see others running for their lives as if they were actually at risk. The video ended shortly after.

"So, now I ask you once more, why did you send fifteen people to the hospital?" The officer said again with an even larger scowl on his face.

I still didn't believe what I had seen. Even if it was me on the picture, it couldn't have actually happened. I didn't even have the backbone to tell someone of the torment I had endured at Shane's hand. There was no way I could have orchestrated such an attack.

"I don't even remember any of that. I honestly don't, and do you really believe someone like me has the ability to attack so many people at once? I mean it's crazy," I said, starting to feel my headache fading and my anxiety taking its place.

The officer rolled his eyes before speaking again in a somber voice of remorse. "To be completely honest, I don't. But the video proves it. That was obviously you in the video, and there isn't any way to fake that."

"But I'm telling you that wasn't me!" I yelled trying to salvage whatever chance I had to plead my obviously absurd case.

"Then who else could it have been?" the officer said in an increasingly sore tone. I hope you realize I can put you in prison for a multitude of assault charges." he paused sighing once more in the process. "However, as much as I want to see that happen, this was a first offense, and someone already paid your bail. So, come with me and we can end this already." The officer then stood and led me out of the room.

Throughout my slow escort to the front room, one question stayed in my mind. Who was it that bailed me out? It certainly couldn't have been my mother; she always worked till ten and couldn't get time off even if she was slowly dying. That only really left one person, mostly due to my father's death before I could remember and my grandparents when I was eight. The person who bailed me out had to be my mom's new boyfriend, Jerry. The problem with this though was that it was for all the wrong reasons.

My mother had met Jerry when I was thirteen, and all from the start I knew he wasn't a good person. He was always obsessed with how we all made him look, striving to change how we both acted to better his own personal image. Needless to say, it normally didn't end well for us. Normally me.

Once I figured it was him, my anxiety spiked as I thought of what he would do once he saw me. I was led out into the front room, and sure enough, there he was. He looked up and smiled, clearly putting up an act.

The officer released his tight grip on my arm. "Now I legally will have to inform you that if an incident like this happens again, we will not hesitate to lock him in a cell." He told him. Jerry nodded in an unhesitant manner.

"I understand, and I can assure you this will not happen again," he told the guard who then turned and walked away, leaving just him and I, alone together. Just like every time he had laid into me for pretty much no reason. Without saying anything, Jerry nonchalantly grabbed me by the wrist and began to drag me out of the police center.

Once he knew no one was watching, Jerry gingerly grabbed my arm and pulled me outside. His mood immediately changed when the door closed. "Look here boy, I don't know what that thing was, and I don't care. I don't like it," he said in a stern voice.

"Jerry, I don't know what's happening either, and honestly, I'm really freaked out." I said trying to make him listen to me. A part of me knew his sheer vainglory would prevent him from doing so though. I felt my heart beating faster, like a drum being incessantly beat on.

Jerry's eye twitched as I spoke. "Frankly, you should be freaked out. That video is all over the internet. I'm already getting calls about from people I'm in good standings with asking what happened. Do you have any idea how this affects me, or how this makes me look? After all the work I do to make our image spotless you go and ruin it."

"Just listen a second!" I yelled, trying to get whatever words I could get out of my breath.

"I bet you don't even know what you've done," Jerry continued to spout out, ignoring my plea. "I swear if we weren't in public, I would thrash you within an inch of your life, but just wait till I get you home," he said.

At that point I couldn't take it anymore, and gave up to my fear. I blacked out once more only hours after it had happened first.

When I came to, there was an even worse sight than before. I saw Jerry groaning, strewn over the bushes, his car flipped over, and I was being restrained by two officers. I was so scared, I just… gave up. I closed my eyes and waited for them to drag me back into the building, but after nearly ten seconds, they didn't. In fact, I even felt their grips loosen a bit.

I opened my eyes to see that neither of them were moving, they were just restrained in a passive state. I looked ahead to see a man dressed in black jeans and a black shirt riding a motorcycle of the same color. He held a weapon which looked like a compact pistol. I looked back at the officers, studying what might have happened. They had almost completely let go of me at that point. I noticed a particularly small, blue dart. I recognized it from a documentary I had seen only a couple days before. It was a new military grade stun dart made for capturing hostages. It worked by releasing a non-malignant neurotoxin into the bloodstream which slowly relaxed the muscles and caused the target to pass out. I immediately wondered how he had one, and then worried that he was a CIA agent or something.

"You're probably feeling scared, weak, and anxious right now, but just know that I can help you. Come with me, my colleagues can help you control that demon. All you have to do is grab my hand and join me," he said to me, outstretching a hand.

Some part of me told me to go with him, but another told me to run. I chose to go with plan B. Without looking at the cyclist, or anyone else around me, I pushed past the officers who then collapsed onto the ground. A part of me didn't care, and the other was too scared to protest. I ran into the woods in front of the police station.

I ran as fast as I could. The little voice in my head kept yelling *'Stop, what are you doing? Do you even realize that he only wants to help?'* I didn't let it stop me though. I continued to run until I was out of sight and far enough to scream out and never be heard.

2

After blacking out and finding that I single handedly caused mass destruction, twice, the last thing I wanted was to accompany someone I didn't know to somewhere I didn't know either. I continued to run through the forest to escape the cyclist, trying to escape whatever monster I had turned into. Though it wasn't long until I found myself lost in the dense forest, unable to find where anything was.

I was in complete solitude, hearing only the swaying of the branches, the cawing of the crows, and the howl of a wolf. The first snowfall had happened the previous day, blanketing the ground in pure white powder. A thin, hooded jacket was the only thing keeping me warm. It would be hours before I was in any kind of danger of freezing, yet something inside me sensed a certain danger in the moment. A certain voice yelling at me to go back.

The only thing you will find here is danger around every corner. Turn back and return to your pursuer. It's for the best.

The voice in my head attempted to convince me of my mistake, but I didn't listen and continued to run through the forest, until I heard a sharp whistling sound. The gentile wolf howl softened and turned to a growl, growing in volume as I went along, until I realized how close the wolf was to me. I walked past the next tree only to see the attacker right in front of me.

In sheer terror, I turned and began to slowly walk back. I stopped still once I saw a new wolf appear, staring at me with its menacing blue eyes. In time, more and more wolves appeared, one after the other until I was surrounded at every angle. They all snarled at me, slowly stepping forward in unison, cutting me off with every step, and with every step my anxiety rose. I didn't want this to be the end of my life, but with nowhere to run, it wasn't like I had a choice. Slowly my vision became blurry and darkened. I slowly felt my body go limp as I began to lose power once more. I felt myself begin to black out.

Just before I lost consciousness though, I faintly heard the roar of an engine revving. Immediately I snapped out of the beast's trance as the figure of a motorcyclist appeared in the shadows atop a nearby hill. Every wolf who had previously stalked and attempted to pounce on me looked up and ran away, leaving me alone and in shock. I looked around at the wolves who were running into the tree line from what I assumed to be fear, then at the cyclist. He was the same person who had put the cops asleep. The person I had ran from. He once again revved his engine and slowly rode down to me, leaving its treads in the snow. I was stunned to see how fast he had found me, especially since he had to maneuver his bike through the tree canopy, avoiding the paths of heavy snow-mounds and ice.

"You know, I really am trying to help. All you have to do is come with me" he said once he finally caught up, riding idle to me.

"You may have just saved my life, but that doesn't tell me anything. None of this has made any sense whatsoever. You just show up out of the blue, scare away some wolves and then expect me to follow you to wherever. You are insane." I said trying to deter him.

It took nearly ten seconds for him to speak to me again in his normal, calm voice. "Where can you go than. It's not like you can just go home, you're a fugitive. You'll be found in an hour, and it's not like you can run forever. There are officers all over the country. You need to face the facts. Face the facts that if you don't come with me, you will soon enough be captured. All you have to do if you wish to avoid this is grab my hand." I could hear the sincerity in his voice, and he did make a point. By now word probably got out that I had escaped, and cops would be swarming everywhere around the city. "This is your choice. I can help you, but it has to be of your own doing."

He was right, at this point I had nowhere else to go except with him. "Okay, I'll go with you, but it's only because if I say no, you'll probably get off of that motorcycle and beg me on your hands and knees." I told him, reaching out my hand to be pulled up onto his bike.

"Thank you for finally understanding, I assure you, you will never regret this decision." He said, revving his motorcycle once more. "These days though, people call me Ryder." His name was incredibly ironic, especially considering that this guy just showed up on a motorcycle out of nowhere.

From the back of his motorcycle, I was driven deep into the forest for nearly twenty minutes until we came to an open cave in the side of a small clearing. "This is where me and the others call home. It's not much but it's sufficient." Ryder said while getting off his bike.

"Wait what? What do you mean others? What are you talking about?" I asked not wanting to get off the motorbike.

Ryder looked back and laughed. "I could take the time to explain everything to you, but it seems to be better to just show you." He turned back and began walking into the cave. "Come on, everything's inside." Somehow this coaxed me to step off of the bike and follow him in the cave. The inside wasn't fancy, just the entrance to an ordinary cave, though probably the only place in the entire forest without snow piled on the ground. There wasn't anything important, but Ryder continued to walk through to the edge of the small cavern and pressed his hand against the rock wall. Immediately a light came on, revealing a handprint scanner inside the wall and a false door in the corner of the room. It was well hidden but a keen eye like mine could spot any hidden detail like this.

Ryder proceeded to walk over to a hidden retina scanner next to the door, and finally pulled off his helmet. This was the first time I had seen his real face since he had saved me. He had eyes the shade of water in moonlight and black hair that cascaded past his eyebrows. This mixed with his strong jawline made him completely rugged. If he had gone to school with me, every girl would be all over him.

Turning back to the wall, Ryder scanned his eye and stepped away. After five seconds had passed, the door opened revealing a corridor going deeper into the cave. The walls pulsed a blue light as if they were made of metal carrying electricity. "Wow, you are full of surprises, aren't you? What else are you hiding from me." I said letting out a slight laugh.

Ryder looked back at me and smirked. "I tend to think of it as being a man of mystery, but if you want to call it that, feel free," he said, brushing his hair to the side and taking a step down into the hallway. "Come on, the others are right down there." He began to gesture me to the blue lit stairway. I followed with little hesitation, taking the lead.

The corridor led me down to a room reminiscent of a living room. There were three others in different corners. The first was a teenage looking girl sitting on the couch in the front left corner typing on a computer. Her speed could have been compared to a top-rated hacker in his own prime. I looked at her feet to see numerous burns on her shoes, as if she had walked through flames while wearing them.

The second was a woman looking older than the first (probably around 10 or so years) in the back-left corner sparing with wooden targets. Based on her form she had been doing this for a while.

The third and final person was a male who seemed to be in his mid-twenties. He sat with his back against a bookshelf in the back-right corner, a book in his left hand and a ball of solid static electricity floating in his right.

"Everyone, I finally found him," Ryder shouted so everyone could hear. I saw each person stop what they were doing and turn to look at me. Each of them seemed incredibly pleased with Ryder's actions. "Welcome to the Guardian Agents Ronen," I heard him say from behind me. "We all have abilities that have made us special. We have been tracking you for the potential of possessing a power like us for nearly a month."

His words seemed to be true, and it made sense how he was able to simply appear out of nowhere ready to save me. It still didn't make sense how I would have gotten some supernatural power. It made no sense why I would have something like this, even if it had laid asleep inside me from birth. "We were trying to recruit you before your power got out of hand, but thankfully it was because of this that we were able to pinpoint your location." Ryder finished, closing his introduction of his team.

I nodded trying to allow the information to sink into my head. "So, who exactly are these people?" I asked trying to get answers. Ryder was just about to tell me when the girl sparing in the back of the room let go of her weapon and approached me. She smiled as she grasped my hand and shook.

"Nice to meet you Ronen, I always love to see new potential." She let go of my hand, allowing her amber hair to drop past one of her eyes. As she dressed it once more, she spoke again. "My name is Ruby. I have knowledge over any and all weapons I can get my hands on."

The sweet and yet fierce girl smiled meekly and gestured to the chestnut-haired girl on the couch staring at her laptop. "That's Cinder over there. Her mental agility outmatches anyone ten-fold, she also has heightened stamina, so she can run for as long as she desires and calculate a plan for battle in seconds."

She then pointed to the boy next to the bookshelf. "And that's Jack over there. He has the ability to create and manipulate static electricity without thought. He just sees the image in his head and the energy just appears out of the air and into his hands."

I had only just met them, and yet they seemed so nice, as if I they had known me their entire lives. It was strangely comforting.

I stood in slight awe knowing that there were others like me. "I guess it's nice to meet you Ruby. It's nice to meet you all in fact. I'm so glad to know that there are people trying to help me." I said as Ruby turned back to her training.

Cinder looked up from her computer and raised an eyebrow to me. "So, you're the one who turns into a demon? A total berserker, but it needs work." She turned back to look at Ruby who had entered the small training studio again. "I got to say, you have your work cut out for you Ruby if you're going to whip him into shape."

Ruby looked back and smiled, "I'm looking forward to it. Once you choose a weapon of course," She told me.

"And Jack back there has years of experience on the human anatomy under his belt. He can get to the bottom of your power, in time though." Cinder said as she turned back to her computer and continued typing. I really felt like all of them cared about me, even if some of them seemed reserved. It was almost as if they were part of my own family.

"Well Ronen, rest up tonight and we'll begin your training tomorrow," Ryder said to me. I could tell that these people would go to hell and back just to help me. For the first time in quite a while I felt truly cared for by someone who wasn't my own mother.

I had no way of denying his request for me to stay. It was late and after releasing the beast twice in a matter of hours, I lacked any energy or initiative to escape. I simply nodded and continued on.

Jack showed me to an empty sleeping quarters down another hallway from the common room. It was honestly not the worst bedroom that I had seen in my life. Small yet quaint, in one way or another it was better than my own room.

"I'll see you tomorrow Ronen." Jack told me, leaving the room. The door seemed to almost close automatically. But I grabbed it before it fully shut.

"Jack, wait up a second." I said. I heard his footsteps turn and walk back towards me.

He opened the door wide enough to walk through, and stood in the doorway. "Yeah, what's up?"

I had too many questions that would fit in the case, but there was really only one which I absolutely needed an answer to. "What's going on? What happened to me today?"

Jack sighed. He seemed earnest, but I could tell he didn't know how to answer me.

"It's kind of complicated to explain in short. Just know that you'll be in good hands." He turned to leave again. "See you tomorrow Ronen."

I nodded as he walked away. The door seemed to shut automatically when I let go of it, and I was left fully alone.

For a moment, all I could do was think of what I had gotten myself into. I had read books of super heroes and had always longed to be like them. To have one thing that made me special, and I actually had it now. Yet I had no way of thinking of it, and to some extent it only seemed like yet another source of stress.

I took a deep breath, looking around the room lit up in a blue tint from the walls. A real light was hung from the ceiling, making the room look completely normal. A person seeing only the inside would have no knowing that the room was built inside of a cave system.

I felt completely normal here, almost at home. It was as if all the stress and anxiety seemed to have fled from my body, and I only felt content, as if those feelings were eaten by the beast himself.

I laid down in bed, retelling the day to myself. "To think only this morning, I was a normal, miserable teenager and now I'm some sort of demon," I quickly became silent, pondering on what I had just said. "Ha, I'm a demon," I said to myself, laughing. I knew something big was about to unfold in my life and to be honest, I couldn't have been more excited.

I laid back in bed and drifted to sleep, my mind filled with anticipation and happiness.

3

The clock read 6:30 when the girl was awakened by her mother. Normally she enjoyed the benefits of sleeping till noon and doing pretty much nothing for the rest of the day every time Saturday came. But lately due to the bombs raining down, she could never sleep. This day was different though. This day, the sound of the bombings slowly grew louder. With the war raging on, no one ever realized any impending doom. In a way, it was pretty tragic. Everyone simply became sitting ducks, unaware that the hunters crouching over them.

The mother of the young girl quickly ran into her room to wake her. "Ruby, Ruby wake up." The girl wretched at the sound of her mother's voice. She shook the girl again. "Ruby, wake up. We have to leave."

The girl of only sixteen soon got up after tossing slightly once more. She was reluctant at first, her mother was prone to paranoia very often. It wasn't uncommon for her to say that they needed to leave their apartment. "Mom, you've woken me up six times in the last month, how is this any different?" She asked her, still rubbing her eyes to wake up.

In the process of looking behind her shoulder repeatedly, the girl's mother spoke up. This time even more anxious. "I just know. This time my sense is just... stronger." She held both hands on her daughter's shoulders. "Please, just listen to me. We need to leave now. Grab your sister and meet me at the door."

Ruby nodded with slight disbelief. She didn't fully understand how her mother was able to sense the incoming danger, but something inside her knew this time, her mother was not lying. Slowly, Ruby walked into the adjoining bedroom. The walls changed from Ruby's favorite shade of red to that of sky blue and cutesy animals. Inside was a small crib holding her eight-month-old sister. As she entered the room, the sound of a bomb echoed around her, enveloping the entire room. Normally the sound would be very faint, but this one was much louder, so loud in fact that it caused the infant to wake up and give off a sharp whine resonating over the sound of the blast.

Ruby walked up to the crib and reached for her little sister. "Yeah, I know that was loud, but soon, we'll all be away from this hell." She uttered to try and sooth the baby's cry.

Ruby immediately walked back into her room for only a moment to grab her favorite book. It was a first edition novel that her father had given to her before he left to fight. The war had taken so many lives, yet Ruby knew he was still alive. He always had a way of surviving any kind of situation he, or his family, had gotten themselves into.

Before leaving her room for the last time, Ruby turned to look at the empty bed. Though she had stayed there for a very short time, she felt as if she had lived there her entire life. It was as if the room had been her home even before the move had happened, and now she was about the leave it... forever. She took one final look at the rest of the cramped room and, with the hand she used to hold her book, flipped the light, forever darkening it and walked to meet her mother at the apartment entrance.

Once her mother was at the door, her and Ruby walked out of their apartment. Looking into her arms, she noticed her mother holding a picture frame. She didn't need to see the photo inside to know that it was of her father who she hadn't seen in nearly a month.

As the two of them walked down the hallway to the stairwell, yet another bomb sounded, creating an ear-splitting crash and causing the baby to start crying once more. "They're getting closer. We have to move now." Her mother said in a voice that was both frightened and commanding. Ruby continued to worry about what she would face on the outside and in the next minute or so, she would be there.

Once outside their apartment, they were unable to mistake the multitude of planes flying above; one in particular had flown in and dropped a bomb on top of the nearby building just as fast as it had flown off.

The explosion occurred just as quickly as the plane had retreated, and the shockwave was enough to send both Ruby and her mother to their knees.

At once the building's windows before the foundation crumbled from the bottom up, only leaving a large pile of steel, cement and dust in its path. Ruby couldn't look away, a horrified look plastered on her face. "Mom," She said with her voice quivering in fear. "Why are they turning on us? When we moved here, we were promised safety from the bombing."

For long seconds her mother did nothing but stare at the wreckage left by the long-gone plane, a horrifying look also stuck to her face. A tear soon fell down her cheek as she told Ruby, "I… I don't know. I wish I could make all of this just stop… but I just can't. All I know is that if we don't leave here, we are going to die. I know I've been wrong in the past, but you just have to trust me. This time I'm right."

Ruby turned around and faced the outskirts of their tiny, minute town. It was always quaint, meant to be kept hidden from most, and before this moment all Ruby did outside of school was return to her apartment and listen to her music. And all that she had complain about was the absence of even a single tree in the ever-expansive desert. But she had no time now to think of such things. She had already witnessed every part of her life; the home she had come to cherish crash into nothing but a pile of rubble.

Ruby didn't have a choice; it was either try to survive or die all together. She followed her mother to the outskirts of the demilitarization zone. Even to go to school she had never gone this far for anything. Everything she needed was in that colony, and now she was forced to watch as everything she had known for the last two years was destroyed.

Turning only a second to see the rubble that was at one point her apartment building, some part of Ruby knew she could no longer run. Turning back again to face the desert, she noticed a strange figure just over the horizon of the new rising sun, but as it grew, she realized what it was. "Mom, we have to leave now." She yelled pointing to the shadowy figure growing by the second.

Grabbing her mother's arm, Ruby ran behind what looked like a closed down mini-mart. Once she gave her sister to her mother's arms, she placed a finger over her mouth and slowly inched around the building. Once she turned the corner, she saw two soldiers surveying the area. They both wore all white uniforms and white face masks. She was prepared to go back around and get her mother when...

"You know, you don't need to just stand there." One of the soldiers said to her. Even though the sound of collapsing buildings was still going on around her, his voice seemed surprisingly clear, and penetrated every part of her, as if It hadn't even come from the owner's mouth. Yet still Ruby did not move from around the corner. "You can stand there for as long as you want but you'll have to move at some point." The soldier once again said in his surprisingly clear voice. It was this that warranted Ruby to slowly step out into the open. She did nothing but scowl at the soldier who smiled. "There you go. You know, you're a resilient one aren't you. Perhaps... especially resilient

"I have no idea what you're talking about." Ruby said while changing her expression to a confused look.

The soldier carefully took off his mask revealing a man with only one eye showing. The other was covered by an eyepatch. "It's actually quite simple. You see, I believe you have something we want, so if you please cooperate, I promise no one will be hurt," he said, giving a smile less sincere than before and more sadistic than ever, leaving Ruby completely lost.

"What kind of thing are you looking for exactly?" She asked as the soldier gave another smile identical to the one before.

"I am so glad you asked. What I am looking for is an amulet about yay big." The soldier said while holding out his hands about two inches apart. "Now please cooperate with me so we won't have to resort to violence. After all, ..." he started to say then whistled for one of his colleagues who came from around the mini-mart, restraining Ruby's mother and holding her sister in the soldier's arms. "You wouldn't want to see your poor mother die."

Ruby could do nothing but watch as the soldier put her mother on her knees with her arms behind her head. He proceeded to them walk back and deliver Ruby's sister to his partner's arms. "How cute, she even shares the same eyes as you. She'll make a wonderful addition to our cause. Now tell me... where is the amulet? The soldier said in a very commanding tone.

After realizing what was happening, Ruby was silent for almost a whole minute, only speaking after a tear ran down her cheek. "I don't know. I'm sorry, I wish I did… but I just don't"

The soldier nodded solemnly. "I understand miss Ruby." He looked back at the soldier standing behind her mother. "Kill them both." He said as he signaled with his hand, turned and walked to his jeep still carrying Ruby's sister in his arms.

"What?" Ruby shouted as the soldier held his gun to her mother's back… and pulled the trigger. Not even a second after a small pool of blood was created around her stomach which spread throughout her shirt as she fell to the ground. "No!" Ruby yelled as she ran over to her side. "Mom… Mom, don't do this. You can't die. Please I can't live without you."

Ruby's mother slowly flickered open her eyes to look at her daughter. "I'm sorry Ruby. I tried to help us all escape this, but I've failed you. The soldiers will take away your sister and possibly kill you. I am already dead. There is no hope for my escape. Just remember this though, I love you. You are the strongest person I have ever known, and for as long as I am still alive, I will hold on to hope that you will survive. Just hold onto hope and I promise you will survive. I know we will see each other again, but I don't want that to come any time soon. Survive… and save your sister."

Behind her sobbing face Ruby nodded, holding onto every word. In her heart she was wishing that she could turn back time. Yet, something tore her back to reality and reminded her there was still a chance to save her sister. As her mother closed her eyes for the last time, Ruby rose to her feet and stared at the soldier who had ordered her death. He held a somber look on her face. "I didn't want to do that. I really didn't," he said, turning to put Ruby's baby sister into his jeep. Once she was secure, he turned back to Ruby, a more impatient look on his face. "I will give you one more chance. I suggest you take it. Where is the amulet?"

Ruby's jaw fell open for a moment then set a face of pure fear and disgust. "I already told you. I don't know." The girl who was at one point full of smiles began to seethe with rage. "You monster. I swear you will pay for what you've just done," She yelled as he waved his hand to signal his partner. It was then that she distinctly heard the cocking of a gun once more.

"As much as I would love to stay, I really must be going. I wish you the best of luck on making it to the afterlife miss Ruby. Goodbye," he said as he hopped into the front seat of and started up his jeep.

Ruby felt a slight tugging at her heart. *I can't die. Not yet. Not now. I'm getting my sister back,* she said to herself, reaching the deepest parts of her soul... and awakening something she never knew about. Just as she finished the words a sharp chill radiated up her left side to the bottom of her arm. Instinctually she knew what it was. Immediately she leaned back and raised her arm into the air.

Less than a tenth of a second later, the sound of the gun firing went off, shooting a bullet through the opening she had made. Ruby found herself unable to breath, but she couldn't stop there. She turned around and thrusted herself forward, pushing her hand to grab the gun from out of his hand, and throw it to the side. Still without stopping she once again lunged forward, throwing a right hook to the soldier's face. This stunned him for a moment. Enough time to slam his face down into her knee.

The soldier stumbled for a moment, but then pulled out a large saber from his belt. With a split second, he pushed forward and slashed down on Ruby's arm. Once his brutal attack was ceased the soldier retreated, giving Ruby enough time to duck down and grab the small pistol she had tossed to the ground seconds before. In a single quick motion, she pulled back the hammer on the gun and aimed at the soldier who had tried to attack first by rushing at Ruby, brandishing his sword. Ruby froze for a moment as she pulled the trigger, releasing the bullet and killing the soldier instantly.

"I refuse to lay awake. Hear my prayer, I am not going to just die!" Ruby yelled, brandishing both arms in the air. "Hear that, I'm not scared of you!" She breathed in, and then out finally. She did nothing but stare at the soldier's lifeless body; killed by her own hands. She stood there for minutes until hearing the unfamiliar voice of a man.

"You know, I have never seen someone fight like that. Your form is almost perfect... almost as if it's more than just skill. More than anything human. Something that must have been given to you by God himself. However, though you have unlocked this power, you lack the discipline necessary to fully utilize it."

Ruby turned around once again to see what looked to be a twenty-year-old man. He had black hair, blue eyes and features that made him attractive to her. His face was discerning and for some reason, just looking at him made Ruby the calmest she had ever been. The man held out his hand for her, and she grabbed it without even having to think.

"Are you going to help me?" Ruby asked the man in a meek tone, looking into the horizon where the soldier had disappeared along with her sister. "They took my sister and… I don't know what I'm supposed to do."

The man nodded. Ruby could tell he had full intent to help. Just not how.

"I'm sorry about your sister, and your mother," He said in a consoling tone. She hadn't told the man about her mother's death. But based on his sudden appearance, she simply assumed that he had watched the entire situation, unable to interfere. "A good family bond is more important to life than anything else in it."

Ruby paused, relaxing from his soothing voice. He was a complete stranger to her and yet it seemed like she had known him forever.

The man continued, "I can't promise that you'll save her, but if you join me, I can guarantee that you'll be strong enough to find her again."

Ruby nodded. She had already made her decision when she had grasped the man's hand. "Okay. I want to find her. I will save her."

The man nodded, and without saying anything else, he pulled her arm and led her away from her old life; where everything she knew came crashing down. In such a grim time, she only felt hope. Hope for herself, and her family.

Slowly, the man led her to a motorcycle parked behind the mini-mart where Ruby had hidden her mother, meaning he had shown up after the lead soldier had left. The young adult man gracefully hopped on the bike and once again held out a hand for Ruby to join him, but before she could grab it, he pulled back.

"Before you join me, just know that once you step on this bike, your entire world will be destroyed. In its place will be something beautiful, but you will never be able to return the person you once were." He said once again holding out a hand for her.

Ruby took only a second before answering, "I have nothing left to go back to, so... I might as well." Ruby said, grabbing his outstretched hand and getting on the motorbike. "By the way, what's your name anyway?"

The man smiled as he put on his helmet and started up the bike. "My name..." he began to say over the hum of the motor, though he did not speak again until he began to travel off into the horizon. "My name... it's Ryder."

4

I awoke as the alarm clock rang at 7 am, shaking me from my fever dream. It seemed comical, but transforming into a demon twice in a single day could really drain a person's energy.

While rubbing my eyes I walked out of the room I was given and into what I had to assume was to be a common area. On the couch just as she was the night before, I found Cinder still typing on her laptop at an astronomical rate. "Are you still hacking on that computer?" I asked her. I didn't want to simply use the word hacking, but my exhaustion prevented me from communicating a better word.

She looked up and gave a very snide smile. "For your information I happen to be in the process of entering your information into our database. Oh... by the way, what's your height and weight." She asked while continuing to type at a much slower rate.

"That's a little personal but... I guess, five feet, ten inches and one-seventy-six pounds." I didn't know the exact number but I felt like it was a good ballpark estimate from what I remembered.

"Great, thanks." Cinder began to say but paused to resume her high-speed typing. "You know, Ruby won the coin flip on you for today. She's over in the kitchen if you want to speak to her."

In the next room I could hear someone cooking. The smell of eggs began to permeate my nose, making my mind race to figure out what was being made. Then I began to wonder about what Cinder meant by telling me of Ruby. "You're trying to shoo me away aren't you."

Cinder continued to type as if she was taking a type of steroid. "No, no I just wanted to tell you that-" Cinder stopped typing all together, looking up from her laptop. "...Wait, what were we talking about?" I could tell that she was too focused to give me a decent response.

"You were saying something about Ruby." I said attempting to jog her memory. Sadly, it was to no avail though.

"Oh yeah, Ruby is in the kitchen if you want to talk to her," Cinder repeated, tuning me out as she once again looked down to her laptop. As she did, I simply decided to go to the kitchen to see Ruby like cinder had suggested... twice.

I walked past the doorframe to see a woman facing the stove, cooking while listening to the radio. I looked closely to realize that she was also dancing to the hip-hop music that was playing. It was as if she didn't even realize that anyone else was watching her. "Hello?" I said with a puzzled look on my face.

Ruby shook in surprise of my sudden appearance. She pushed a single button to turn off her music and turned to face me, a smile remaining on her face. I notice the braid she had her red hair in swung around her shoulder. All of her long hair was put in a single tail. It was very familiar to me. I distinctly remembered it from a book I had read in the sixth grade. This braid looked almost exactly identical.

"Morning Ronen. Lucky for you I won the coin flip against Jack, so for today I'm putting you through my own personal boot camp. Of course, you're first going to have to choose a weapon. That way, I can teach you everything you need to know to master it." She told me, leaning forward on the kitchen island. She had said a lot, but from what I heard I was going to learn how to fight. Naturally, it excited me.

"What are you cooking?" I said while looking over towards the stove, prompting her to turn around once more, grab the pan she was using, and place its contents on a plate.

"I made French Toast, one of my best recipes."

She placed the plate in front of me, the smell continuing to waft my nose. I hesitantly took a bite of the food she had made and immediately could taste the many flavors melting together in my mouth. It reminded me of all the meals my mother had made for me ever since I was a kid. It was so reminiscent that it nearly reduced me to tears while I was eating. It was by far the best thing I had ever tasted.

"Okay… this is amazing. How did you make it?" I asked her between bites.

Ruby smiled about twice as big as I ate. "Not telling, the recipe dies with me, but I do add nutmeg to it." She told me, picking at the food on her own plate. "So, tell me, do you have any previous experience with weapons of any kind."

I thought back to all the points in my life when I had learned any type of weapon. Most of the time I learned how to use different axes in scouts, but I never learned any kind of use as a weapon. Even after I had reached the highest rank. "I learned how to use an axe, but never to fight. Other than that, no nothing."

She nodded, listening very intently. "With the right kind of training, those skills can be transferred to axe fighting. Seems like a good place to start with. And who better to teach you than the person whose power is literally knowledge over all weapons created by man."

It was at this point when I remembered the dream I experienced the previous night. I had no idea if it was real or not, but it seemed to show how Ruby had first awakened her power just as I had the previous day. It seemed to be tragic too. Something that no person would want to relive again, but I still asked. "Hey Ruby…," I began.

She looked up with a clear face, eyes soft. "Yeah?"

I bit the bullet and simply asked. "When you were first growing up. Did you… have a sister?"

Ruby's eyes doubled in size as the words left my lips. She dropped her fork on the plate and lightly gasped. I could see a fleck of flame simmer in her eyes. "How do you know that?" She asked, holding back what seemed to be anger.

Even though I knew I had struck a nerve with her, I answered. "I... I didn't. I mean not really. It's just... I had a dream about it last night. I just didn't know if it was real or not." I said trying to avoid her stare. She certainly didn't seem happy with my question, but not like she didn't want to answer. "Well... is it?" I asked.

Ruby sighed, and reluctantly, she once again spoke. "It's true. I'm not proud of it, but I did have a sister when I was younger." The fire in her eyes burned out, doused by water beginning to form. "What did you see?"

"She was taken by a military man in an all-white uniform, but I don't know who he was."

Ruby nodded solemnly. "I figured as much. Huh... if you must know I will tell you." Her eyes began to water once more even before she began to speak. "This was all before I had formally joined the Guardians. Back when I still lived with my family in a Syrian demilitarization zone. My father was part of the army, so I only saw him about once a month. I never felt like I was in any danger, despite all the bombs I heard going off... constantly. The thing is, as you saw, eventually they got closer, cornering us. The man you saw wanted me to give him something. He said it was some kind of amulet. Obviously, I didn't have it, much less even knew what he was talking about, and in return for it, the soldier did the unthinkable." Her story was naturally something she would want to keep hidden, but she seemed surprisingly calm. Instead of waiting for her to continue, I decided to continue with what I saw in the dream.

"So, what I saw was true?"

Ruby once again gave a solemn, straight face. Again, she slowly nodded her head. "All of it. I watched as my home was destroyed, my mother killed, and my baby sister taken away from me. Since then I've vowed that I would rescue her. But even if I were to save her, I have no clue if she would listen."

I couldn't help but interrupt, "So you don't have any idea where she is?"

"No... I do, the problem is getting to her." Still Ruby remained calm. Not a single tear was shed despite everything. "I understand if you look at me differently now. It just... needed to be said."

I shook my head in desperation, "No... no, not at all. In fact, I kind of understand. I never truly knew my father growing up. I only knew my mother being hurt by her other boyfriends. She worked hard to support the both of us, even if it meant being completely miserable. And that's not even beginning to mention me." I ate the last bit of food from the plate, savoring the incredible taste once more. "Heck, just last week I was stressing out because of a single test. Looking back, I can't believe that someone could be so stupid."

"Yeah... I get it. Life can be tough. It's full of challenges for anyone. Ryder says it best though. The strain that is exhausted on a person is proportional to the strength of their power. In other words, the more that you live through, the stronger you become in mind, body and even the soul" Ruby said finally smiling. "It all depends on how you deal with it though." She finally began to perk up, lightening the mood of both of us. She didn't seem the least bit naïve despite her young adult look, like she had already lived through everything the world could give her. In a way though, she really had.

I had lived nearly my entire life knowing only my mother, never truly remembering my father's face. I wouldn't know what to do if I were to lose her, but Ruby did, and I assumed she hadn't seen her father since then either. At that point, only Ryder could have helped her become who she was on this day.

"Anyway…" Ruby began once more knocking me out of the sudden trance. "It might be a good idea to start your weapon training early, so we should head out." She said while standing from her side of the kitchen island. I followed without saying another thing.

As Ruby and I began to walk through the opposite doorway, Jack walked in, wearing a smirk larger than I had ever seen before. "Just remember Ruby, I've got him tomorrow. So, don't work him too hard today."

"Come on Jack, today I'm only teaching him the basics weapon training. I have to build up some muscle before I get into the challenging stuff." Ruby said before turning to me and giving a warm, fierce smile. "Now that's when the real fun starts." I sighed thinking of what she could have me do, grinning in the process. "You'll thank me in a few weeks." Ruby said as she ushered me out of the kitchen. "Come on,

I'll show you the armory, then we can get down to the basics."

"I'll see you tomorrow Ronen." Jack said as Ruby began to walk through the doorway he had come from.

"Don't worry, he may seem scary, but it's just an act. He's actually quite sweet." Ruby told me prompting a large sneer from Jack. Ruby looked back at him and smirked. "Like I'm wrong."

"Still. You could let me have a little fun." Jack said as Ruby and I left the room.

Ruby led me deeper into the bunker, crossing corridors almost like a maze until we reached a small room where every wall was covered shelves full of different types of weapons. Ruby began to cross the shelves looking for the desired weapons. "Let's see, one handed swords, battle staffs, spears, oh... here we go, axes. Go ahead, pick one you like." She told me. I walked up to the shelf spanning up to the ceiling. Every axe looked different. Each style was there in every possible color. I looked over the entire shelf and decided to choose a dark iron battle axe with a metal handle colored green and gray. It was clearly a well-crafted tool, but a deadly weapon in the arms of its user. Slowly, I picked it up from its stand only to realize it was much heavier than I had expected, almost forcing me to drop it at first glance.

"Don't worry if you can't lift it yet. With my help, you'll gain muscle very easily." Ruby told me.

I smiled and lifted the axe with both hands. "So, what are we starting with?"

Ruby picked up a random axe and turned back to me. "There's a training ground outside. The dummies there are made of a material durable enough to take an axe strike. I can start your first lesson once we're there."

"Really… there's outdoor facilities. I thought you were supposed to stay as hidden as possible."

"We are, but the field and part of the forest outside are hidden from radars. As long as we stay in the perimeter… they won't find us." Ruby told me while walking out of the armory. It was strange, but she used the word 'they' as if I knew who she was talking about. I didn't understand what she meant at the time, but whoever 'they' were, they seemed important enough to avoid.

*   *   *   *   *

Once Ruby and I exited the bunker and walked into the cave, I finally noticed just how beautiful the outside field was. The sun cascaded past the tree line to make a breathtaking work of art. All the snow from last night had since gone away, still leaving the crisp air in its wake. "The training ground is just past that ridge over there." Ruby said while vaguely pointing in a direction out the door.

I began to walk out of the cave and walk to the right only to hear Ruby's sarcastic voice once more. "Other way."

I turned around and began walking in the other direction, pretending like nothing had ever happened. By this point Ruby had closed the door and began to walk in the right direction. "So, before we start, could I ask you something?" I asked as we walked.

Ruby looked back with a consoling look on her face. "Go ahead what is it."

"Earlier you said 'they' would not find us, and last night Ryder told me that anywhere I went, 'they' would find me. Who are 'they' exactly?"

Ruby stared back with a puzzled look on her face. "Is that what I said? I guess sometimes I slip into vague speech. It's probably because I'm closest to Ryder. I was actually the first to join his Guardian team you know."

"So, does that mean there are more Guardians out there?" I asked while continuing to walk through the ankle high grass.

Ruby turned back before answering my question. "Of course. We are only the Guardians for this given state. There are also multiple potential Guardians out there, and those who have powers but don't use them. We don't take prisoners here. As long as they don't cause any problems, we don't have to get involved."

"So, the only reason I was brought here last night was because I was found by the police when I first transformed?"

"Precisely, when we first found you as a potential Guardian, Cinder set out to pinpoint your location. Lucky enough you lived in the same town as our bunker. Anything farther and Ryder probably would have had to break you out of jail."

I wanted to continue talking and get all the information I could but settled for what I had heard when I saw what I figured to be the training ground. It was simply a square space in the grass with a wooden floor, smaller weapon racks, and 3 leather practice dummies all lined up on one side. A single bench was also placed in the grass for possible viewing.

"So, you said that you used axes for lumber purposes. Am I correct?" Ruby asked me while leaning over one of the training dummies. I nodded without saying anything else. "Perfect. Not many people understand this, but a lot of the concepts of recreational use and axe fighting are essentially the same, with a few differences in speed and coordination. Here let me show you."

I watched as Ruby grabbed her axe and took a fighting stance. I looked close at her eyes to see them being glossed over in a silver shine. I had no other choice than to assume that was her power at work.

In a single burst Ruby thrusted her entire body forward toward the target. Once she was in range, she pulled her arm around her body, hitting the target in the stomach. Then, she quickly pulled the axe out of the dummy and spun the axe around her head, thrusting her body around a second time. She once again did the same for a third time, only this time she switched the hand she was using and hit the dummy on the opposite side.

As she pulled the axe out of the hard-leather dummy, Ruby once again began to speak. "You see, when fighting with an axe, it's important to focus not only on speed or thrust, but also core balance. You need to manage your core as you spin as well as anticipate when you will hit your target. That way you can connect multiple hits in rapid succession of each other while giving you the chance to anticipate your opponent's next move as well."

I stood in front of her, mouth agape at the marvel I had just seen. It seemed simple enough, but I had no idea if I would be able to recreate it. Ruby stepped away from the practice dummy, giving me space. "Now you give it a try. Just visualize the opponent before you, concentrate on the target and remember, keep balance."

I gripped the axe in my hands and stepped a few feet from the dummy. Then, trying my hardest to concentrate, I threw the axe over my shoulder, and thrusted my body forward.

Trying my hardest to keep balance, I spun and threw the axe into the dummy's right side. Then, just like I had seen Ruby do, I spun the axe around my head hitting the dummy in its head. However, once I pulled the axe out a second time, I stumbled and fell beck, slamming on the wooden floor.

Ruby grabbed my arm to pull me back to my feet. "Careful kid. Remember what I said, your core is everything in fighting. If your balance fails, you're going to fall. Then again, it's not like I expected it to happen on a first try."

I grabbed the axe from off the ground and took another stance, trying to succeed in the three-part attack once more. This time though, I wasn't even able to get the axe past my head before once again tripping. Then, a third time and even a fourth time, I still couldn't finish the attack.

"Okay, I have an idea," Ruby began to say after helping me to my feet once more. "Close your eyes and try to focus on the attack movements. Visualize the axe being thrown into the target."

Following her word, I closed my eyes, trying to imagine the attack, but no matter what, all I could think of was my mother. What would she think when she found out about what happened the previous day, or that I had run away? Jerry wouldn't have to spin the story to make me seem like the villain, he just needed to tell it like it happened. After all, it was me who kicked him into the bushes and somehow flipped his truck.

I took a stance, clearing my head. *Enough feeling sorry for yourself,* a voice said to me. My hand twitched and while keeping my eyes closed, I thrusted forward, hitting the target once, twice, and finally… a third time. I had finally completed the attack. I was overjoyed as I opened my eyes to see three new chinks in the leather practice dummy.

"I did it. I actually did it." I said to Ruby. I turned around with a smile to match her gasping look. "What?"

Ruby was practically biting her fist. "Your hand. Look at your hand." She told me in a tone that was almost shrieking.

I looked down to see that I wasn't holding the dark iron axe that was in my hand a moment ago. Instead, what was there was a translucent, full jade green axe. Immediately I threw the thing on the ground in a shriek. A few seconds after hitting the ground though, the axe shattered into a multitude of shards that were soon blown away by the wind. "What the hell was that thing." I yelled to her.

Ruby, still with her hand to her face, did nothing but stare at the place where the weapon had dissolved into nothingness." I… I don't know. It's nothing like I've ever seen before. Almost as if… but the chances are so astronomical."

I looked back at her, eyes bulging. "What, what is so unlikely to happen?" I yelled once more.

Ruby finally took her hand away from her face and told me. "Sometimes, when a person possesses a powerful enough version of the Guardian gene, they can manifest multiple powers. I have only seen it maybe twice since I awakened my power, but I think this is the case. Those axes seem to phase in and out of reality at your own will. We may have to investigate them."

I looked at the hand that had created the axe. "Well, at least I can sort of control this power… I think." I said with a laugh. I looked right into Ruby's eyes, studying her face. In multiple ways… she was just like my own mother.

5

"Wait a second, are you saying that you suddenly have a second power?" Cinder asked as I told her what had happened in my training only a couple hours ago hour before. I honestly doubted if I even could explain it right. I didn't even fully understand it.

"That's one way of saying it... I think." I said trying to remember what Ruby had said verbatim. "you see, the Guardian gene I possess is apparently strong enough to support a second ability."

Cinder looked back, impressed for the first time since I had met her. When I came back from the outside, she had closed her laptop, giving her full attention to me. Although, it was obvious that that part of it was in another place. "It's still better than the power that I have."

"Don't you have a second ability too?

"Not exactly," Cinder quickly responded. "If anything, it's an extension. A major boost to endurance and stamina, both in mind and body.

Anyways... what about yours? You mind showing off for a minute? The best power I've seen so far is Jack's static, and other than being a decent power supply, there isn't much of a practical use. So, come on... seriously let me see."

As a single word exited my mouth Ryder walked in, leaning against the doorway without saying anything.

"If I could I would love to, but this is pretty much the same as my original power. It just... comes and goes as it pleases." I said, watching Ryder's face form a smirk.

"Huh... how funny, I thought you would have mastered that power by now." He said with slight sarcasm.

"It's only been a day... did you expect me to be shooting lasers from my fingers or something?" I said, slightly amused.

Ryder slowly shook his head. "Of course not, you're too nice for a power like that." At that point he was unable to hide his chucking. This of course caused Cinder to let out a slight giggle in return. I just grinned and continued to listen. "But in all seriousness, it seems as though your problem is a simple lack of information. You don't know a single thing about why you have your power in the first place."

"Is that all? Is it really that simple of a problem?" I asked with slight discontent. It just seemed strange how an ability like mine would be controlled by such a thing as information. Even something as simple as the axes.

Ryder nodded with great adamance. "Cinder was the exact same way. I still remember when she joined seven years ago. Rather than being able to control her enhanced agility, she twitched uncontrollably. It was so cute."

Cinder rolled her eyes, reverting to her look of opposition. "For the last time Ryder, I was twelve and I have ADHD."

Ryder once again laughed, "And look at what you've become now. Only ten years and you've all but mastered your power. Sometimes people train for double that and don't even get halfway." He turned back to me, "It does seem like your problem is mostly what you don't know though. There's easy fix to that though."

Up to that point I hadn't considered how much there was really to know. Most powers are self-explanatory from the moment you receive them, and through all of Ruby's training, I could only imagine how I got the Guardian gene in the first place. "Please don't tell me I need to study a giant book or something. I've never been good with that kind of thing." I exclaimed.

Ryder held his hand to his chin for a moment while looking off at the wall behind me, not even quivering his lips. "I don't think I've actually ever considered writing our history down, but that's an idea for another day. What I was going to suggest was that I give you a crash course in what being a Guardian actually represents."

"Do you really think that that'll be enough." I still didn't think a simple conversation would work as well as he said. It just didn't seem possible that such a problem could be solved with simple words. It just didn't make sense.

He began to walk past Cinder; towards the stairwell I had entered through about half an hour before. "Come with me and I guarantee you'll understand how to use your power. The secondary one that is."

Before I left, I heard cinder yell to me. "And I expect to see that axe you spoke of by tomorrow morning."

*   *   *   *   *

Ryder led me in the opposite direction that Ruby had before. Out into the open field we had walked through the previous night. Other than the change in light and the melting of the morning frost in the now beginning to set sun, nothing had changed. I was able to point out a rather large stream flowing from the tree line. A small hillside overlooked the entire scene, almost as if it was calling to me.

"Beautiful, isn't it?" Ryder began to say from behind me, his shadow casting next to mine. "This is one of the best places for the view alone. It's almost as if this hill is the true embodiment of the word serenity."

"It is," I replied still staring at the scene at the bottom of the hill. "But what does the stream have to do with me being a Guardian?"

"Isn't it obvious," Ryder said as he led me down the hill to the stream, and while sitting down, dipped his hand into the fast-moving water. His hand immediately began to push back with the current.

Though the water seems inviting, the power of the current is strong enough to knock you over, thus making it much more than it ever seems. The same is true for the powers of a Guardian gene."

Ryder slowly drew his hand out of the water. Yet I still felt as confused as ever. "I don't follow you. Are you saying that a Guardian's power is completely random?"

"Not in the slightest." He said reassuringly. "let's try this, have you ever looked at someone and thought that they were the total embodiment of a single word? Like... when you look at Cinder, what word comes to mind?"

I thought of the chestnut-haired girl who I had met the night before. She was sweet in her own way, with times of sass like any other young adult. She was attractive and very intelligent. I could tell that she was well taught from the moment I first spoke to her. More important though, every time I did talk to her, she was behind her laptop, working. I didn't even know if she needed sleep. She was by far the most hardworking person I had ever met. "Diligence. I mean... she hasn't stopped working on that laptop since I met her." Ryder slowly nodded.

"Exactly, and it's because of this this that she was granted her enhanced mental agility and stamina. The thing is, every power works the same way. All our powers... or at least the primary ones directly relate to who we are. Though, some are a little vaguer than others." I couldn't help but think what that meant for him. I had a good understanding of everyone else's abilities but knew nothing about what

Ryder could do. It was almost as if no one else knew, or he didn't want me to know.

"What do you mean by that?" I asked him while staring down at the rushing water.

Ryder as well looked back into the water and spoke again, while holding up his pointer finger. "For instance, the many years I've known Ruby has led me to believe that her personality can be considered the embodiment of hope. However, it still has eluded me on the exact reason why that resulted in her advanced weapon proficiency."

"Wow so does that mean if the personality fits, a Guardian could have the ability to manipulate anyone in an instant?"

Ryder shook his head discerningly. "That's impossible. While the overall chances for the Guardian gene is vast, there are two types of powers that will never be seen. A Guardian will never have the ability to travel back in time, and they will never have the ability to control the will of other people."

I looked past the stream and into the dense forest. "Oh. So… what about me. What word do you think I embody?"

"Actually," Ryder began once more. "It's quite simple. Your power can be considered to be the transformation into that beast creature. With such an unstable force being kept in someone who lived their life fearing the future, I'd say that it's safe to guess that you represent control."

What he said made absolute sense. Throughout my life I had always been keen on controlling my environment. I was always very organized to the point where I had developed an acute sense of OCD. "I figured as much, but how does knowing that help me understand the demon form?"

Ryder stood up from his spot by the stream, looking away from my face to try to find an answer. "Normally, people who take control of a multitude of situations possess little control of their own emotions. That could be the key to your power, learning how to level off your anxiety. From what I saw at the police station yesterday, the beast emerges when you reach high enough levels of fear or stress. It would make sense that the only way to control that is to learn how to keep those emotions in check. Right now, that transformation is a crutch, and you will continue to use it as a crutch until you learn control of yourself."

"And I'm guessing only then will I start to control that monster?" I asked, receiving a slow nod from Ryder "Is that why I'm training with Ruby?"

Ryder shrugged, "You could say that. All new recruits are required to be taught how to use at least one type of weapon, which Ruby takes care of for obviously. She taught cinder everything she knows, and she can more than defend herself. Those axes you create though, are different than anything I have seen before. It's impossible to disarm you because they can phase back at will. I don't know what it is, but I sense a great power in you, more than any Guardian I've ever seen... including me."

Some part of me knew he would say something like that, the overused line that by now can only be considered cliché. "So, let me guess. It's imperative that I learn how to master this power as soon as possible." I said looking back at him.

Ryder once again took a second to think and then nodded. "Pretty much, but there's no need to say it so bluntly. But anyways..." Ryder stopped looking back at the horizon. "The sun is about to set. Can I say that my job was completed in the allotted time?" he said brushing a flap of his hair out of his eyes, fully revealing them.

"You could say that," I said, smiling. "but if the sun is starting to set then we'd better head inside." Ryder nodded, turning and beginning to walk back to the cave entrance. Immediately a question flashed in my head, and I began to think of what word Ryder could represent. I quickly set it aside knowing I could never get the right answer. I could tell these people had multiple secrets. Some of which I couldn't even hope to uncover.

I looked in my hand to see a multitude of green shards begin to form. They began to swirl in the pale air, but didn't manage to bond together to form an axe like they had in my training. Instead, they simply collapsed and blew away in the breeze. Even still, I smiled, waiting for what would come next, knowing one thing: this power, both of my powers really, could be the one thing to lead me out of the hole I dug myself into throughout my entire life.

6

If there is one thing that I will always say I am most afraid of; it would be restraints. I could never understand the idea of being powerless to do anything and just allow someone to prod around my body. The thing is, I never thought I this fear would be a problem until I heard Jack tell me he wanted to run a couple 'tests' on the potential of my powers.

The morning began just as the last did. I walked out of my room and was once again greeted by Cinder's laptop. She was of course working again, so in the zone that she didn't even notice my presence. I walked in front of her, watching her fingers dance around the keyboard. "Do you ever sleep?"

Cinder halted her typing and looked up for a moment. "Of course I do, my power just makes it so that I only require about half the sleep of a normal person. Most of the time I only sleep about four hours per night."

"Okay, so what are you doing then?"

To this, Cinder turned her laptop around to show an interface which included what seemed to be an innumerable number of code lines. "If you need to know, I'm updating the system on the radar scrambler. It's just something I have to do every couple of weeks so that it doesn't shut down." She said before turning back the computer and resuming her speed typing. Since I knew from experience that was all I would get out of her, I went to the kitchen to see who I would find this morning.

As I entered the room, I found not Ruby, but Jack sitting at a table in the corner of the room. He was eating a bowl of cereal and reading from a folded newspaper when he noticed I was there. He then looked up at me and smirked. "You're finally awake. I was beginning to think I'd have to pull you out of bed myself. But anyways, good morning Ronen."

I saw an extra bowl at a seat across from him and sat down. "Give me a break, I'm a heavy sleeper."

Jack laughed. The kind of laugh that could lighten the mood of every situation. "I suppose that's correct. In fact, I bet you wouldn't have even woken up if I had done such." He folded the newspaper once more and set it aside. "Anyways, I hear Ruby gave you a crash course on axe fighting yesterday."

I nodded slightly, "Ryder also told me about how the Guardian powers reflects the person's personality."

"To tell you the truth though, I'm not very keen on that idea." Jack told me while continuing to eat. "I mean think about it, what part about my personality suggests this." He then proceeded to hold out his hand with all of his fingers pointing upward. Immediately, sparks of static began to fly between the five conduits.

"From what I heard, the present you isn't necessarily what influences your power. It's probably the personality of the person as they awaken the gene." I said using whatever logic I could think of.

Jack sighed while looking at his palm. "Precisely." He slowly smiled.

"So, then what was it. When did you awaken your power?"

Jack closed his hand into a fist, extinguishing the flying sparks. "It's been a very long time. The first time I used it was back when I was... maybe thirteen. About ten years ago. You could say my situation was kind of like yours."

"And you learned to keep it under wraps thanks to Ryder?" I asked him, intrigued at his past.

Jack shook his head swiftly. "Not exactly, to tell you the truth I only joined these people like... three years ago, but I shouldn't really get into the rest. Just know I have a little bit of a dark past." He slid an empty bowl to the side and continued. "As a matter of fact, your power leads to your training for today."

"What do you mean?" I asked with a puzzled look.

Jack looked back at his newspaper and then continued. "In the time between my gene activation and my joining the Guardians, I studied genetic science. This is the reason why Ryder wanted me to help figure out what your power entirely includes, or I guess both of them."

"So how do you propose to do that?" I asked.

Jack looked away to think for a moment. "The simplest way is by studying different cell samples when you are both in and out of your beast form, although a brain scan also may help."

I looked straight at him with eyes of fear. "Really, because I'm not very big on needles."

Jack smirked once more and stood from the table. "I wouldn't worry. If a twelve-year-old Cinder can take it, so can you."

As Jack said this, I could hear the young adult voice from the other room. "We talked about this Jack."

Jack walked over to the doorway. "You don't have to resent your past Cinder!"

Almost as if it was scripted, Cinder quickly yelled back. "Yes, I do!"

Jack laughed again and walked away. "Don't you just love angst." I stood up and walked over to where he was, "come on, I'll show you my lab," he said, walking down the same hallway he had disappeared through the day before. I followed close behind.

Jack quickly led me down another set of hallways to a horror science lab type room complete with beakers filled with unknown mixtures, and the stereotypical table with leather straps. "Hop up on the table and I'll get everything ready." I heard Jack say as he turned to a workbench.

A minute later Jack Turned around holding a needle and two vials. "Lay back," he told me. I did as he said as he strapped my wrists to the table.

"Is this really necessary?" I asked while he strapped my legs into place

"Trust me, you can never be too careful with a power like yours."

Jack took a second to sterilize the skin on my shoulder, and stuck the needle in, slowly pulling out blood from my shoulder. The pain mixed with my anxiety was enough to nearly make me pass out. Instead though, I blacked out, using my uncontrollable power once more.

Nothing had changed when I regained control of my body. Jack had his back to me, studying the sample of blood under a microscope. "So, are you finally calm?" He asked looking over his shoulder.

I scowled at him. "You know I hate it when that happens, and I still don't know how to control it."

A minute later Ryder ran into the room. "What the heck was that?" He asked, looking around the room to see that nothing had changed. "Seriously, what was that scream."

Jack fully turned around from the table. The look on his face showed clear intent. "Yeah... I might have activated Ronen's beast form or something, but look at this," he told Ryder as he walked over to the microscope. Ryder shook his head and walked over to see what he meant. "I took two samples, one normal, and the other while he was in beast form. Notice the intense discoloration between them. I mean one of them is nearly black. The amount of adrenaline that had to be pumping through his body is simply astonishing... I mean really, to cause deoxidization to that extreme would require an amount that I previously assumed to be inhuman."

Ryder pulled away from the microscope, first looking at me, then at Jack. "There is definitely no disguising that, but I hope you realize how foolish that was of you Jack."

Jack looked back in complete confusion. "What do you mean? This breakthrough clearly shows how Ronen's power changes his body down to the cellular level. How is that foolish?"

Ryder walked over to the table which I was still strapped to and undid the bindings holding my wrists in place. "It might not be the best time to say this, but at this phase Ronen's power could very well be fighting for control of his body. It's like that with all transformation abilities. The more times he turns without control, the more control the beast takes."

Jacks eyes suddenly widened, as if he had just reached an epiphany. "If that's the case, do you think he might be the next user. The descendant meant to finally make use of the relic. The one written in the tomb."

I looked at both of them one by one as I undid the straps on my legs, freeing myself. "What are you two talking about?"

Ryder sighed as I stood from the table, "I suppose you have every right to know. That's not a bad idea to try out, so follow me. I'll explain on the way to the archives." He then began to usher me out of the room but turned once more before leaving. "Jack... just try to do something constructive.

"Aye aye captain Ryder." Jack said. I looked back to see him bridge static between his fingers.

Ryder quickly led me even deeper into the bunker, so far that it made me wonder how long it actually took to make so many tunnels. "So where exactly are you taking me this time?"

Once again, Ryder sighed before answering. "Let me first explain with a little story. About three-hundred-years ago, in an archaeological dig, a group of scientists unearthed a Guardian's tomb holding nothing but the body, a single relic, and a prophecy inscribed on the wall. It stated that there would come a day when the Guardians would be tested. An unmistakable evil would awaken, and it is only our job to subdue it, otherwise it's power would consume everything we know about this world. But the writing also spoke of hope, prophesizing a Guardian could save the Guardians from certain demise." He stopped, raising his hand to my shoulder. "Ronen, since we found out about you, we suspected such but were reluctant to take this step. You see… once you choose this path, there is absolutely no chance of returning to your old life."

Like everything else Ryder had told me, there was a lot to absorb. People already knew about the moment I first transformed, but there was still a chance I could still return, and everyone wouldn't believe what they remembered. My anxiety didn't want to believe the idea that I was part of the prophecy, yet something inside me knew there was no other choice.

Trust me, the voice said from inside my soul, *this is your destiny.*

"My old life ended the minute I first took on the beast form. There isn't any reason for me not to dig deeper down the rabbit hole that is your society." To this remark, Ryder nodded, and opened a door to his left marked 'relics'.

I entered alone, waiting for the door to automatically close. "You should recognize the item when you see it, that is, if the prophecy is as written. I trust you'll choose the correct one." Ryder said behind me as the door shut.

I searched around the room looking at all the relics laid on open displays. The first I saw was a pair of gauntlets studded at the wrist with jewels like diamonds and rubies. It looked spectacular, but I knew it wasn't what I was looking for. After staring at it long enough, I began to realize how flashy and crude it really was. It couldn't possibly be the relic I was after.

The next display I moved to held a silver cloak laced with silk. Like the gauntlets it was elegant and beautiful. However, that was all it was. The cloak held absolutely no capabilities in battle. So instead, I moved onto the next display.

The third relic wasn't at all as flashy as the others. It wasn't encrusted with jewels or threaded with a beautiful material. It was just a Metal necklace fashioned into the shape of a shield. The only thing that seemed flashy was the chain-link chord sprawled in the back of the display. It was simple, but there was something about it that also seemed humbling.

Unlike the other relics though, my perception didn't change with time. It had to be the one I was meant to choose.

I picked up the slender necklace from the stand and placed it around my neck. Once the shield emblem hit my chest though, the entire shape began to glow. It slowly began to morph into a different shape. That of a cross with six bands, one on each of the four sides and the remaining two intersecting in the middle. The chain link lacing also changed to a black nylon looking material.

It seemed strange though why the shape would change to a cross. In certain periods of my life, my mother had taken me to church, but not enough that I could consider myself to be a very religious person, even though I kept the moral code of one. That still didn't hide the fact that this was the relic I was meant to choose. Once the transformation was complete, I felt a wave of passivity wash over me, removing my previous anxiety and fear, making me calm.

I walked out of the room to see Ryder still waiting in the hallway. I had barely taken five minutes to make my choice, so he hadn't gone very far. He looked at my neck to see the newly transformed amulet. "If anything, this is proof that you are in fact one of the descendants we are looking for. That cross will repel the demon inside of you until you see fit, and then it will become your strength, but you should still be able to use your axes," He began to say before ushering me away. "Just remember, that cross loses its power once it leaves your neck, so the main priority is still controlling your power. Needless to say, you will still be training with Ruby, and maybe even Cinder at some points."

I paused for a moment. I didn't know what it was, but it seemed almost like he had too much knowledge on the topic of the Guardians, like he had been around much longer than he had led on to be. "Ryder, if you don't mind me asking, what power did the Guardian gene give you?"

Ryder stopped in place and looked at me eye to eye. "Do you really wish to know?" I nodded, though slightly skeptical. Ryder once again sighed before continuing his tale. "As I said before, that amulet was found about three hundred years ago. However, I never said that one of the men to find it... was me. I possess the power to reverse the aging process, bending my own health at will. Though I am not one of the original Guardians, I am a closer descendant than any other still alive."

Once again, I took a minute to process What he had told me. "Wait a second, what do you mean by original Guardians? I thought the gene was a genetic mutation."

Ryder shook his head. "You're mistaken, the guardians date back all the way to Egypt during the Roman Empire when the original seven Guardians were born, and in the time of need, God bestowed them with abilities just like ours which they used to protect the civilization from demise. Their descendants possess the same gene they did. The proof of your descendance though, is right on your neck." I looked down at the necklace to hear him continue. "That very amulet belonged to the original

Guardian Aaron of Cairo. A Guardian with the power of augmentation. Only his descendants can use the relic he was given."

After he told me this, we continued to walk to the surface. I found the information to be very interesting, and with the relic I had just received, I had absolutely nothing to worry about. "I hope you realize that from now on, your training will increase in difficulty now that we don't have to worry about you not being able to control your power." Ryder said.

I nodded. "I already figured that out." I said with a smirk. At last, I finally felt like I had finally taken a step in the right direction.

7

"Keyah." Ruby yelled a triumphant war cry as she pulled her sword to match her pivoting motion. Her speed was one that was faster than anyone I had seen before in videos, but at this point it didn't even cause me to flinch. To block her advance, I phased dual axes into my hands and sliced up in the opposite angle. The sword was pushed out of my way with a resounding 'clang'

Ruby smirked as our faces passed each other. I lunged away to create a five-foot gap between the two of us. Slowly I released my grip on the axes, allowing them to disappear into shards that slowly blew away into the breeze just as Ruby pulled a whip from her waist. She cracked the slender weapon forward allowing me little time for reaction. I tumbled to the left, falling out of the whip's path. Ruby repeated the action, continuing to crack her whip without hesitation. Once, twice, three times, only finally cutting my cheek on the fourth attack.

I held a hand against the cut to subside the searing pain. With my other hand I phased into existence another axe which I used to block her fifth attack. The whip wrapped around the shaft allowing me the opportunity to yank the weapon out of her hand. I took my left hand off of my cheek and gripped the top of the handle where the whip was wrapped and pulled back with all the power I could muster.

As soon as the whip began to tighten, Ruby released her hands, pushing me back on the ground. I looked up from the ground to her smirk, which had burst into laughter. I shook my head and gave a snide grin. "Okay, okay I give," I said gasping from the extreme training I was put under.

Ruby slowly strode over to where I laid and offered a hand. "You're improving," She said.

I looked her straight in the eyes and gave another snide smile. "You know I probably would have won that last match if it weren't for the fact that my opponent is literally the most experienced fighter alive."

Ruby pulled mt to my feet, her face clad in the same smile she had always hit me with. "Oh, please if I were to start you off easy there would be no chance of you learning even close to this fast. If it makes you feel any better, you are improving. I had to use my power at full force to win that last fight. You really do make a good sparring partner."

I smiled back at her. "As I said before, I learned from the best." I looked around the at the fighting studio. There were a few leather dummies to one side, a small rack that could only hold maybe five or so weapons, and a single bench which was right behind where I had stood. "It's hard to believe I've been here for three weeks. It feels like a lifetime."

Ruby nodded and turned to rack her sword. "Well, the daily training will do that to you, but in time it becomes habit. Just wait until you're put out in the field. Then you really find out the brink of life, and yourself."

She was right. I had only scratched the surface of my power or even the Guardians themselves. I still felt dazed and confused. Just as the little girl named Alice did as she fell down the rabbit hole.

Slowly, Ruby walked off of the wooden slab that was the studio floor and looked back. "You coming?" She asked, turning her head but not her body.

I looked at my chest, at the cross I wore. "I think I'd rather stay back and practice a little more, just to cool down a little."

Ruby nodded, pointing back at me. "And that's why I like you. Even when not being instructed you still want to learn. Take as long as you need." She turned and continued to walk toward the bunker. I looked back as she turned the corner and disappeared out of sight.

Turning back to the studio, I pondered on my training. "It really has only been three weeks." I looked down again and clutched the cross around my neck. "How long is it going to take until I learn to control you?" I paused for a second realizing the truth. "What even are you?" I asked myself. My own power was something I had never known about before it had first activated. It made me scared to think of its destructive power. So much that I hadn't taken the chance at taking off the amulet for the entire three weeks I had it.

"They're restraining you; you know." I heard a voice say from a distance. I quickly turned around to see an adult man approach from behind. He looked to be in his mid-thirties with slightly gray hair and sunglasses the same color. I noticed he also wore a blazer, jeans, and a gray undershirt.

In terror, I clutched the cross tighter and phased a single axe in my remaining hand. "Who the hell are you?" I said taking a guard stance.

The man smirked and held up his hands with innocence. "Woah, easy there. I didn't come here with any malice intents. I merely wish to offer you a proposition." To his words, I slowly lowered my axe, but did not release it.

"Thank you. It's always nice to have a simple chat between two civilized people. You can call me Maxwell. I wish to warn you of the people you are currently with. All they want to do is restrain your power. They're afraid of it, and they only want to use it for their own selfish needs. I wish to ask you to come with me. I can teach you the full extent of your power." He slowly moved his hand to push my gaze away from his face and looked straight at me with consoling eyes. "I can make you great." He said while holding out a hand.

I thought about what he had said. If he was right, the so called 'Guardians' were trying to keep my power hidden, and they would never help me with it. But from what I had seen in the past three weeks, this was something I simply could not believe. "You seem nice, but I just can't abandon my friends." I said to him.

The man seemed to be surprised at my answer. "I implore you to reconsider." He said in a tone that was more demanding than before, but I still shook my head.

He looked down, and pulled out an extendable cane from his blazer, which he proceeded to lean on. "Very well. A small part of me knew she was right. But there was always the chance I suppose. This is why I came prepared for such a moment." He said as he walked closer to me, lifted his staff close to my face, and pushed down on a button. Once he did, a small puff of red smoke shot out in my face. Within seconds, I felt my head begin to cloud and my legs going limp.

"What...was that?" I said in a haze as my body collapsed to the ground.

Before I passed out, I saw Maxwell squat down to my eye level. "I hope you realize that this all could have easily been avoided." Those words repeated in my head. Those final seven words continued until I fully lost consciousness without releasing my power.

*   *   *   *   *

It was around noon when Cinder returned to the bunker from her morning run with Jack behind her, looking as if he was about to pass out. "You know, I don't mind slowing down for you. As long as I get the exercise it's fine." She said, not even showing any sign of being the least bit winded.

Jack glared at her while walking into the kitchen. "No… this is… how I improve… my stamina, … I need water." He said in an extremely breathy voice, gasping after every couple words.

He crossed Ruby as she walked out, strait to Cinder. "Didn't you walk past the sparring studio on your way back?"

"Yeah," Cinder answered. "Why?"

Ruby nodded, still keeping a slight look of distress. "Was Ronen out there? He said he wanted to stay back about an hour ago, but he still hasn't come back."

Cinder shook her head in confusion. "I didn't see him, but if you want, I can tap into the camera footage and see where he went."

Ruby nodded and watched as Cinder opened her laptop and began to lowly scrub through the video footage. "Now all I have to do is go through the video feed until we see Ronen." She said as she began to rewind the video. She stopped at an hour and ten minutes prior and they both watched as Ronen was drugged and carried out of the area by a man they both knew all too well.

"This is not good," Ruby began. "Here it was my responsibility to keep Ronen safe, and he gets captured the first time I leave him alone. And of all the people it just had to be him."

Ryder walked in from the kitchen with a confused look on his face. "Cinder, how many times do I have to tell not to overwork Jack on your runs, and what guy are you talking about?" He asked. To this, Cinder rewinded the video and showed Ryder what they had just seen. His voice stayed calm but used a darker tone. "How is this possible Cinder. Your satellite array was supposed to shield our presence. How did he find us?"

Cinder began to open her satellite program and review her program. "I… I just don't know. I thought my program was unbreakable… but he just, found a loophole somehow." She said in a panicked voice.

"How are we going to get him back? Even the four of us can't even think about going up against him." Ruby said in the same distressed tone. "Oh, why did I have to leave him alone? This should never have happened."

Cinder placed a hand on Ruby's shoulder consolingly. "It could have happened to any of us. Don't blame yourself, otherwise we've already lost. It may seem impossible, but we can get him back. Even if we have to deal with them again." Cinder looked up at him and nodded, a small bit of water forming in her eyes.

Ryder pulled out his phone and began dialing an unseen number. "If he's truly the one we're dealing with, getting Ronen back is our number one priority." He put his phone to his ear and began speaking. "Yes, hello. This is Ryder Kertez of the United States Guardians Oregon branch, calling for backup. Get me agents Parker and Brittany. Serpente is back again. I repeat, Serpente is back."

Ryder slowly closed the phone and tuned to once more face Cinder and Ruby. "So, what now?" Ruby asked with remorse.

"Well," Ryser began to say with a minute bit of worry in his tone. "It looks like we're going on another retrieval mission, and our target is once again... Ronen Haven."

8

The feeling I had waking up in a drug haze was that of someone with a hangover getting hit by a bus. My splitting headache was so strong in fact that my vision began to blur. I was barely able to notice the room I had been placed in. It was a simple cement walled room with only a single light to illuminate the entire space. The only thing inside the room though, besides an open door was a single cot which I woke up in. I slowly stood to the ground to feel a sudden burst of nausea.

I suddenly sat back down on the cot. "Well, that guy is either a highly trained biologist... or a giant stoner." I said to myself as I managed to successfully stand up. With the searing pain still pelting my forehead, I walked out the door, holding my head in an attempt to vitiate my earlier nausea.

Once I was in the hallway, I noticed multiple sounds assault my ears. The only ones I could recognize though were fists hitting a heavy bag, metal being grinded against stone, and metal rings clanging together. Obviously, I chose to approach the first noise as the others would only increase the pain of my aching head.

The sound slowly led me down the hallways and eventually to an indoor gym much larger than the training studio the Guardians had, and just as I had suspected, there was a boy repeatedly hitting a heavy bag. Like me, he seemed to possess massive amounts of strength. But from what I saw, he also had discipline. A will to fight that drove his passion. I walked into the room as he turned, revealing his face to me. He had supple features, slick golden-brown hair and bright green eyes. What came as a surprise to me though, was how young he was. He didn't seem much older than me, maybe only a year or two. Yet he seemed like he had years' worth of training.

He clearly didn't know me, but he still smiled. "Well, look at that. Master Serpente said that your dose would last eight hours, yet here you are after only six. I got to say, you're messing with a lot of the higher-up's plans." He said to me with a glaring look and hints of contempt. "I guess you can stay If you wish though. I'm just taking some time to practice my technique."

I slowly pulled my hand away from my forehead and down to my chest, but to my great surprise, my cross was missing. Gripping my hand where the charm used to be, I stared at the kid for several seconds. "Where… where am I? And… where's my stuff?"

The boy smirked, almost laughing. "I can't tell you how many times that's said when people wake up here. It's almost cliché. You get used to it though." He stepped back and grabbed a particular weapon I had never seen before. It was a circular blade with a bar used as a handle in the middle.

I slowly felt my headache begin to lessen. "That doesn't answer my question. If you're not going to tell me, I can go to the next room," I said, beginning to sneer. "And what are you holding?"

The kid rolled his eyes and continued to laugh. "Yeah that's not a good idea. The other members aren't exactly as inviting as I am. If you don't want to stick around, the best thing for you to do is go back to your room and wait for Master Serpente or miss Morris to get you." He proceeded to raise the weapon in his hand. "As for your other question, this is my weapon of choice, called a chakram. Watch, it works just like a boomerang."

I took a step back and watched the kid took a stance almost like he was throwing a frisbee and threw the disk-shaped blade. Slowly the blade turned and flew to a dummy a couple of meters away, strangely losing no speed as it flew through the leather, cutting off its head. The chakram then abnormally turned back to the thrower, flying straight to his hand, which he caught without effort. I stood shocked, mouth agape. "Woah, that was almost inhuman. How did you do that?"

The boy smirked as he pulled back once more. "A good bit of it mostly comes from a lifetime of practice. But you are correct, the rest is inhuman." He moved back to a normal stance and set down his weapon. "Sorry, here I am saying all these things and I never even introduced myself." He walked up to me and held out a hand just as Maxwell had before he drugged me. "The name's Hunter Haines. Around here though, I'm known as the gravity master," he said, shaking my hand. "It's nice to meet you Ronen."

Ignoring the fact that he knew my name, I withdrew my hand and held it to my side. "I guess it's nice to meet you, but what do you mean by master of gravity?" I asked him.

Hunter stepped back and retrieved his chakram. "Actually, it's quite simple. You see, every object has its own gravitational force, even if it might not seem like it because it's masked by the earth's. The denser the object, the stronger the force. I have the ability to tap into that gravity and change it, thus changing its force, like in the throw I performed. Once I throw the chakram, I amplify the gravity of my target causing it to turn, then I amplify my own pull to bring it back."

I nodded in almost complete understanding. "So that's your Guardian ability. That's pretty nice."

Hunter scowled and rolled his eyes. "You might think of yourself as one of those savior want-to-be freedom fighters, but not me. I belong purely to the Serpent Corps, and once I prove myself, I will rise from the elite battalion and finally get a seat on the high council led by Master Serpente himself."

I could see that he was very articulate, yet he seemed to hold a serious grudge against the Guardians. It was either that or he was taught to hate them. "Anyways…" Hunter began again. "I have to say, I heard about your power and… I'm impressed."

"Really?" I asked him in surprise.

Hunter nodded. "Of course. Pretty much all possible abilities are equal in their potential, whether it be an ability useful in battle, or strategy. Just trust in what you have. It might surprise you."

What he said made sense but didn't exactly make me feel any better. What use would a super power be for if all it does is destroy without control. I didn't understand at all what I could do with it. not to mention how to control it.

Hunter glared above me at a clock hanging on the doorway. "I have to go, and it's probably a good idea for you to head back to your room if you want to stay inconspicuous. I can walk you back if you want." He said as he strutted past me into the hallway. I nodded and allowed him to escort me. The entire time I kept wondering what kind of personality trait would result in the manipulation of gravity. It would have to be something that would in some way influence others, but not control. At one point I bounced around with the idea of humility, but quickly dismissed it. He didn't seem entirely humble, but not prideful either. It was... something else. I would have continued to think but had to dismiss the idea when I was back at my room.

Throughout the entire encounter, I had forgotten about my missing cross. But with the closed door I had no way of looking for it. I figured at this point, the best thing to do was simply reflect and wait for the door to open more. I found it strange how my mind was still clear and my anxiety still passive. Chances were, it was my intense exhaustion, which prevented me from even thinking. It certainly was what prevented me from thinking about anything anymore. I simply laid back and waited for the inevitable to happen.

     *   *   *   *   *

Agent Parker Steel was one the toughest mercenaries in all of the Guardian Fighters. Wielding the power to substantially increase his own muscle mass for short periods of time. He was most known for his fighting approach: making sure to strike first and hard. Meanwhile, agent Brittany Steel, Parker's wife took a different approach. She could be dainty at times, yet also strong and hardworking. She possessed the ability to distort the properties of light, allowing to essentially disappear in dimly lit areas. She preferred the idea of stealth, attacking when others had no idea where she was. However, when the two of them teamed up together, they never left a battle in total defeat. It was for this reason and that they both chose to fight with their own fists that they were nicknamed the unwavering gauntlets.

Along with them, Jack was tasked to act as a guide. "If nothing's changed, the portion of the facility we currently are in is only used for research. It seems empty though." He said while they walked through the hallway of nothing more than closed doors.

Parker raised an eyebrow to Jack's statement. "Research for what? Please don't tell me he's experimenting on other Guardians."

Jack slumped his shoulders in solemnity "I wish I could tell you no. Serpente is attempting to find a way to prematurely activate the Guardian gene. No idea if he's succeeded yet. He kept everything in complete secrecy from everyone not working on his projects. Whether the information be about the findings or a new test subject. The only ones who knew were the researchers and of course, the test subjects themselves."

Once again, parker raised an eyebrow to Jack's statement. "How would you know about it then?"

Jack stayed quiet for a moment, unable to answer. Soon though, he let out a long sigh, and answered. "I... was both. I was brought in as a test subject shortly after I had awakened my power, but I don't really wish to talk about the pain of the tests I was put in. I still have scars from some of them, one in fact was actually from my own electricity. Just... know it made me wish for death, each day."

"That's awful. Like a fate worse than death. I can't imagine living like that for years. Brittany asked from beside Parker. "What happened next?"

Jack continued. "Well, over time, Serpente realized my resilience, so I was moved to a researcher and even joined his elite squadron. Or... his Elite Serpents as the others liked to call it, and I stayed that way until Ryder came along. For five years I fought for him." He stopped and let out another sigh. "Hard to believe it, all that time for nothing. All it did was fuel my hatred for the world."

It was at this point when Brittany advanced to Jack and placed a hand on his shoulder, without saying anything. Jack smiled at her and turned to the next hallway.

"If nothing's changed, the rest of the Elite Serpents members are restricted from these halls." He suddenly switched to a sarcastic tone. "Lest they find out the truth of their god, Maxwell Serpente. I swear their motto is ignorance is bliss."

As the three continued to walk, Jack began to hear someone else's footsteps. The three of them turned another corner to see the face of an olive-skinned girl who looked to be no older than twenty. Brown hair draped across her shoulder like a waterfall. A leather glove was placed on each hand. Four sockets were in place at the knuckles. They were bare and hollow, as if something was missing from them.

Jack's eyes grew wide at the sight of her as she gave a slight grin. "Well, well. Serpente was right. It seems that a couple of rats have managed to infiltrate our facilities. Lucky for him, he has his personal exterminator to get rid of you for him. Prepare to be exterminated, Vermin." She looked over both parker and Brittany, then realized that Jack was present. "Mumtaz [Excellent]. It's not every day I get to exterminate a full-blown traitor to the Serpent Corps." Her sadistic aura could have been felt for miles.

Her smile prevailing throughout her remarks, the girl once more spoke only to Jack. "You know, I bet that if you were to beg him, Master Serpente just might consider taking you back. Provided of course that you aid me in the removal to these other two rats." She snickered while she gave her proposition. "What do you say Jack? Care to join me once more?"

Jack immediately recognized the other language she spoke as Arabic. He did nothing but scowl at her, his eyes filling with rage. "That part of me died years ago Talia, and what remained is what you see today. If you honestly expect me to rejoin your cult, you're just as dumb as you were when I left."

The girl flashed a snide, sadistic smile at all three of them. "Kama tatamana [As you wish]," She began to say in an heir of slight sophistication. Without time for thought, she pulled out two sets of metal claws resembling knives. She continued to speak as she proceeded to clip them into the sockets on her gloves one at a time. "It seems there is yet another rat to deal with. But if I must, I will do everything in my power to complete the job given to me by Master Serpente. Prepare for death… traitors. I'm going to enjoy tearing you to shreds."

Talia quickly popped her neck and charged at parker who quickly held both hands up to block. His muscles bulged out of his skin from his power. She swiped across both arms, cutting a sharp line past the skin, but not drawing blood. Parker released his stance not seeming at all affected by the gash made by his attacker. "You got to cut a lot deeper than that to phase me." He tried to counter her attack with a right hook, but he came short while Talia retreated.

Talia brandished her claws once more, this time aiming for Brittany. She ran to her and once she came close enough, Brittany used the best of her abilities to cloak herself, becoming almost ghostlike. She dodged to the side and punched down on Talia's back, knocking her on the ground for a moment. She attempted to completely cloak herself but could only achieve the same transparency as the had already become.

"There's too much light in here." Brittany yelled to Jack who was still trying to figure out what to do.

"A little bit of a precaution we had installed from the last attack." The young adult brute said as she climbed to her feet.

Parker went in for yet another attack when her back was turned, leaving an opening for Talia to counter, lunging past and scratching Parker's shoulder. To this, he wretched slightly, but quickly turned in an attempt to attack again. As with his fist shot towards her, Talia blocked with her claws, cutting into Parker's knuckles, and then pushing him back.

Parker wretched in pain, shaking his hand to get feeling back. "I can't get a hit in," He yelled to Jack. "She moves too fast."

Jack squinted, as he looked at the calescent lights overhead at the same time that Talia began to shift her gaze to him. And after avoiding another one of Parker's attacks, she began closing the ten-meter gap between the two of them. It was in that moment when Jack finally formulated a plan. Immediately, he began shooting electricity between his fingers until the static level reached his desired amount, forming a ball shape. He then hurled the ball straight in the air, breaking the light overhead. The light shattered into millions of pieces which began to fall in the air like snow, breaking the circuit and leaving the entire hallway in a dim light.

"You think a simple blackout can stop me? I bet it can't even stop a rat like yourself," Talia said with a face unrecognizable in the darkness. She once again brandished her claws and began to charge to him once more. Before she was able to reach Jack, Brittany grabbed his arm, cloaking them both in darkness. He sidestepped to avoid Talia's attack, and once again formed a ball of static which he threw at her feet, stunning her, but not distinguishing her fighting spirit. This was repeated three times until Talia finally fell back, unable to stand again.

Jack let go of Brittany, becoming visible once more, and stood in front of her, grinning. "Nearly five whole years since we last dueled, and you still can't best me. You really should update your workout regimen." Talia laid nearly motionless, scowling at everyone.

"You're a snake! You hear me! You do nothing but poison and infect! That's all you've ever done! But I will not be infected by your lies!"

Parker walked up with a face of pity. "All she's doing is spouting nonsense. You think I should make her quiet?"

Jack held a hand to Parker. "There's no reason to. She won't be able to stand for at least an hour, until the excess electricity is purged from her body. That should give us enough time."

Brittany uncloaked herself and stared at Talia, still on the floor, twitching. "Well then, seeing that we're out of danger, who is this psychopath?"

Jack ceased his blank stare and began his description. "Her full name is Talia Leyva. She used to be a page under the third commander of the Serpent Corps Syria branch until she was forced to transfer to America when terrorists overthrew the country. She has fought for the Serpent corps almost since birth." It was hard to be sure, but Jack was almost entirely sure that he could see Talia smile with pride as he described her track record.

Jack continued. "Her power is flexibility. In a sense, she overcomes the nerves in her tendons and ligaments, allowing her to move her body into inhuman contortions. She acts as the first defense of the Serpent corps mansion, but the others probably won't act for a while, leaving us a window of time to get Ronen."

Talia continued to scow at Jack. "You're wrong, you can't succeed, It's already too late! By now our newest patient is receiving his first test. Ha… He's ours now!" she said with a sadistic cackle.

Parker looked back up at Jack with a sudden concerned look. "How fast can we get to Ronen?"

Jack looked through the hallway, trying to picture the rout in his head. "We can get there in five minutes if we're lucky." he said before all three of them hurried away from the girl who was unable to move.

Just before they were out of earshot, Jack could hear Talia's muffled yell from behind him once more. "And when you see that weapon touting has been, I'm forced to call big sis… tell her that I'm waiting, and I will be victorious!"

Jack stared back for only a moment to process the comment and then left her, still paralyzed on the ground.

*   *   *   *   *

I only had to wait about an hour before the door opened again. I still laid on the same cot I had woken up in before, only now, I felt my senses coming back to me as the drug haze faded from existence. Instead, I could hear the constant clacking of a hard-sole shoe hitting the ground, and inside came a black-haired woman much older than I. She strode in wearing a black pantsuit and matching pumps. With each step, the clacking continued as she got closer.

"Ronen Haven," She said in a slightly honeyed voice. "I have yet to see a child possessing a constitution such as yours. I can already see that you will make a lovely addition to the Serpent corps, and a wonderful prodigy to Dr. Serpente." She then turned out into the hallway. "If you would please follow me." she continued to say in her slightly pleasant tone, that made it seem as if I was about to be marched towards a death sentence.

I stood from the cot and stared into her face. She seemed as serious as humanly possible. "Who are you, and more importantly, what is this place?" I asked, obeying her earlier command.

Without looking down to me, the woman answered. "You are now in the Serpent Corps facility for research and training. As for me, my name is Mickala, but you will please call me Ms. Morris. Now if you have anything else to say, I would prefer it to be short."

In the one eye that was visible, I noticed a slightly blue gloss fall over her eyes. It was only for the briefest of moments, but it reminded me of the silver gloss that came over Ruby's eyes when she grabbed a weapon. "Did you just activate your... ability?" I asked, wondering if she would even answer.

Just as I had believed, the woman named Mickala Morris shook her head. "That, I cannot tell you. According to Dr. Serpente and the protocol of project Hellsing, I am unable to divulge any personal information for the time being." Something told me that would be her answer to every question.

The woman led me down another multiple sets of corridors, so many that I actually lost track of the number. She stopped at a single room marked Genetic Research Room B. without talking she opened the door, and ushered me inside. It was then that she began to strap me to a table just as Jack did on my second day with the Guardians. I thought about resisting, but realized that there really wasn't a good reason to, since there was no way I would be able to escape without being caught. She smiled, admiring her handy work. "Dr. Serpente will be with you shortly. For the time being, sit tight." She said, smiling at her joke. She then left me in the room, alone. I heard the door lock only a second later.

I looked around the room filled with a monochromatic red tint. All I could see from the table were multiple machines I had never seen before, much less knew what they did. I looked up to see a single red lamp hanging from the ceiling, lighting the entire room.

Within a minute, the door was once again unlocked, and the man who had drugged and kidnapped me entered. The man known as Maxwell

Serpente. "Hello again Ronen," he said to me. "Tell me, what do you think of the facility? It's simply spectacular isn't it?" He said in a grave voice.

I glared straight into his beady green eyes. "Do I like it? First you drug me, then you kidnap me, and now you've got me strapped to a table to do God only knows what! You know the worst part is that you think I'm just going to lay here! You're so self-absorbed you think my friends won't care to rescue me! The Guardians are coming! They will save me!" I yelled, beginning to become hysterical, letting out all the hatred I had built up.

Serpente's face filled with nothing but pure rage. He grabbed my neck making it so that I could barely breathe. "Don't you ever say their names in front of me. I will not take slander from a weed like you. Those roaches have been trying to take away the empire I created for years now. If you ask me, they couldn't even think of coming within ten miles of this place, and for all I care that's how it should be. Just know that if you want to act like one of them, I'll treat you like one of them."

Serpente released his hands from my neck and placed them in front of his face, doing a type of breathing exercise. Once he was calm, he smiled again. "Anyways, I am not here to torment you. If I did, you'd already be getting forever chewed by the devil himself. No... in fact, I merely wish to help you."

"Let me guess. It's something you say will help me, but it will only help you blind me from the truth.

Just like you did to that kid, Hunter." I said trying to pull away from him.

Serpente shook his head and chuckled menacingly. "Ha… think about the people you believe in for a moment, then tell me who's really blind to the truth. Face it, you've had your eyes closed all your life, and now that you finally learn the truth, you would rather embrace ignorance. Let me tell you one thing child; you have only bit the skin of the peach that is your destiny." He then proceeded to turn from me, facing a workbench. "And it's my job to show you more. You see, your power is very special as I'm sure you've heard many times before. You possess a force of utter destruction. Like me, you could be a god. Wouldn't you like that, having the ability to strike fear in even the strongest of men. You will never have to take any pain from anyone. You will be a god among men."

He was completely crazy. In my own fear I pictured what Ryder would say in this moment. "All you are is a fool. You're nothing but a mad man. You seek something that will never come to you." I rolled my eyes in frustration. "And I'm the child here."

Serpente breathed heavily, seeming to get ever more annoyed at my aspersions. He turned back with a cotton ball and what looked to be a sewing needle. "A child wouldn't have near the intelligence to achieve even a fraction of my ability." He then proceeded to prick my arm and draw a small amount of blood. He gathered the scarlet liquid in the cotton ball and once again turned back.

"It's actually quite comical. Here you are attempting to assault me with all the fire you can muster, and I'm trying to help you. I almost feel insulted." He said in the same grave voice he had used the entire time.

I scowled at his back, trying to pull out of the shackles, knowing very well that it wouldn't work. "What you call help could very well destroy me."

I could tell Serpente was laughing at me, even though I couldn't see him. "That's just the risk you have to take. After all, it's the only way we can become stronger." Once again, Serpente turned, around holding a syringe filled with a black substance. "Just trust me Ronen. I can give you the truth." He then stuck the syringe in my arm and released the drug into my bloodstream. I immediately felt my mind begin to cloud and my anxiety skyrocket.

"You psychopath! What the hell did you do to me?" I screamed, thrashing in the restraints I was tightly bound to. A seething pain fled down my body. A pain so great there could never be an anodyne for it.

Serpente looked down at me, his eyes almost consoling. "I truly am sorry about the pain, but just be patient. Soon you will unlock something you never could have with those... 'Guardians'." He seemed almost sick when speaking the name of their organization.

I felt my skin crawl as it was engulfed in a fiery sensation. I suddenly lost control of my muscles, every spark of willpower extinguished against the pain. I simply gave up and waited for the moment that I would black out.

Serpente turned away and walked to the door. "I wish I could stay. I truly do, but I sadly have other priorities to attend to with the rest of my empire. Sit tight though, soon you will be enlightened." He then opened the door and walked into the hallway. "So long for now Ronen." He said as he closed the door once again, locking it from behind him.

My entire body numbed as I laid there, waiting for something to happen. I lost track of the flow of time as my mind slowly slipped away from me. I couldn't help but wonder what was going to happen. The demon inside of me wanted nothing more than to destroy and if I let him out, I had no idea if I would regain control again.

Throughout it all there was a single question I asked with all my mind and heart: Would I ever see her again? Would I wake from my own nightmare only to see her smiling face with triumph? The face of my mother.

I stopped my train of thought when I heard the sound of someone pounding on the door. Immediately, the door slammed open, bathing the entire room in white light. In the doorway, was a large, incredibly muscular man. He was accompanied by the silhouette of an adult woman, and when he stepped back, I saw a familiar face step into the room. I laid motionless as Jack unlocked my shackles. "My God, what did he do to you," he said with the most concerned look I had ever seen.

I couldn't move any part of my body, but I was able to speak albeit with minor strain. "He said… he would reveal… the truth to me. What tyrant… would do this?" I said, coughing in between words.

Jack frowned, with empathy. "Yeah. That sounds like Serpente. He's completely despicable." A small tear began to well in his eyelid. The calm and collected person I had seen before was nowhere to be seen. "I'm sorry. This shouldn't have happened. Can you move?"

Once again, I strained to even get out the word no. To this, Jack nodded, undid the rest of my shackles, and lifted me into a fireman's carry. With every movement my muscles burned like acid coursing through my veins. I tried to scream in pain but couldn't get a single word out.

Jack carried me through every corridor, holding me over his shoulder. He walked past a multitude of locked doors while avoiding the wing I had originally woken up in. I paid close attention to a girl who seemed to be paralyzed on the floor. As soon as she saw me, her expression changed form a scowl to a smile. The kind of smile someone gave only when they knew they had won. A smile which showed that she knew we would eventually meet in a more formal way.

Minutes past as Jack continued to carry me through the maze of rooms, until finally I saw the light of the outside. "Hang in there Ronen. Just a little bit further," I heard Jack say. I could barely hold out the will to keep consciousness. The only thing I held onto was the idea that if I gave up, I would once again release the demon.

Jack reached the end of the final hallway and opened the door to the outside. The sunlight against my skin almost felt like I was being stabbed in every pore of my body. A helicopter was placed in the field ready to depart. I watched as the other two liberators boarded first, and then Jack who laid me down on the floor of the helicopter.

Once I was let go of, I noticed the familiar amber-haired girl run to my side, both hugging me, and checking my pulse. "Ronen! What is this? What did he do to you?" Ruby cried, before turning to Jack. "What can we do? How are we supposed to help him?" she asked, frantically.

Jack shook his head in disbelief. Probably hoping that none of this was real. "There really isn't anything we can do. We just have to wait and see if he recovers."

With every twinge in my body aching, I managed to gain muscle control and roll onto my knees. "Huh...huh...what way in hell is this enlightenment? What kind of lunatic is he?" I screamed in pain as blood began to flow through my throat and onto the floor. "Ruby... I'm so sorry. This shouldn't have happened, but a price has to be paid. This will not overcome me." I said between breaths, wiping the blood from my mouth.

Ruby, staying by my side, began to sob as she wrapped her arm around me. "Cinder tell me we can do something!" She yelled to the pilot.

The young, nineteen-year-old turned from her seat and shook her head. "This is a foreign phenomenon even for me. I don't know if we can do anything. We just need to wait and see what happens."

The helicopter started, and I felt my own gravity increase. Ruby continued to sob, even when she stepped away. I continued to vomit up blood for almost half a minute. My body went cold, and my vision was eclipsed by darkness.

I passed out, my will, unable to control my body anymore.

9

Once again, I woke up in an unknown location with no idea of what had happened. I racked my brain trying to remember. The memories only floated back to me in small amounts though. I read them back in my mind one by one.

I was captured by someone named Maxwell Serpente and taken to his research facility.

It was at that point that I met Hunter Haines, the master of gravity, and Mickala Morris, who I knew pretty much nothing about.

I was restrained by Serpente who drugged me with a serum that caused me to lose control of my powers

I was rescued by the Guardians, only to pass out after.

Now I was stuck in a single room of red wallpaper. There were no doors, no windows, and strangely no lights, yet the entire room was visible.

"So, after all this time we finally meet face to face… Ronen" A disembodied voice said to me. I turned around to face him, only to see a sight I didn't recognize at first, but then I realized that I knew him all too well. It was like looking in a mirror. He had the same black bangs brushed to the side as I did, the same eyes, and was even standing with near the same posture. There was one difference though. This person had what seemed to be black streaks going through his right eye, and down his arms. The voice though, was the one thing I recognized most.

"That voice. I… I know you." I continued to rack my brain until I finally came to the full conclusion. "It's you. You're the beast. The, the voice in my head."

The boy smirked to my comment. He seemed to be happy to see me, like he had been waiting. "In the living flesh, and nice nickname by the way. The beast… I love it." he said, letting out a laugh in the process.

I looked back at him, still in surprise. "You're the one who got me arrested."

His face changed from amused to temperamental. "And you're the one who locked me away. For years I was trapped, and then once I was finally released, you chose to once again lock me away."

"Weren't you the one who told me to get the cross in the first place?"

The beast shook his head and scowled. "The power of the amulet was never to lock me away. Why would an item so great be used to dampen? You were just too scared to accept the cross's power. And now the amulet is gone! You've always been too scared for anything!"

I suddenly felt a well of anger form in my chest, and I yelled back. "So, your idea to fix that was to flip a bus and get me arrested?"

"I took control of all your pent-up anger from your entire life. At some point I just lost control and couldn't help but lash out," The beast said. I turned around in a huff to avoid his glare. We both stayed silent for nearly an entire minute, and though I couldn't see him, I knew he had eyes of sincerity. Perhaps even empathy. "You know, we both have a common enemy. Maxwell Serpente is up to something. I don't know what it is, and neither do you, but there's no reason for us to bicker when he's still in power."

I suddenly spun around again. "How do you know who Serpente is?"

The beast raised an eyebrow in surprise. "Wow, I didn't think that would get you to listen. I almost prepared an entire speech, but… yeah, I guess this works too. As for the question though, here." He then waved his hand and turned the wall to his left into a TV screen. On it showed the scene of Ruby teaching me how to swing an axe on my first day. He snapped his fingers, and suddenly changed the scene to that of Jack taking my blood samples on my second day. Then again, he snapped his fingers to change the picture to later that day when Ryder bestowed Aaron of Cairo upon me amulet. To finish, he waved his hands again, making the screen return to the state of a wall.

"I've seen everything," he began to say. "Every dream, every desire, and every mistake that later sparked your anxiety."

I didn't think it was possible, but he did care. He had seen every flaw I had.

The beast held up both wrists, exposing the black streaks from his wrist, to his shoulder, or at least that's what I assumed. "Do you know what this is? Why I have these?"

"They're tattoos, aren't they?" I said giving the only answer I could think of.

The beast shook his head and set both arms down, revealing the steaks on the opposite sides of his arms. "They're scars." He paused for a moment, a solemn face showing through. "Your scars. The embodiment of every moment of pain your life has given you."

It was then that I realized the truth of him. He was never meant to be a force of anger or spite. He was meant to be a force of understanding. A control of emotions. My emotions. That was what he did when I gave up control. He took my negative emotions to make himself stronger, leaving only the strong, passive emotions to me. He had seen and felt every flaw I had and wanted to help. Over the years, I had developed many problems with self-esteem and usually avoided close friendships because of it. Yet, it felt comforting to knew he was there.

The beast continued. "If we work together, you can have more than you can ever imagine. We can have more than imaginable, just trust me." He said holding out a hand to me.

I sighed, but still nodded. "I guess we have a deal then Mr…"

The boy smiled sincerely again. "Xaraxis. My name is Xaraxis."

"Okay. I suppose I can relinquish control if you promise not to do anything stupid… like get me arrested."

The boy smirked again. "Again, not of my own power."

I smiled and nodded. "Then I guess we have a deal Xaraxis. I look forward to seeing what you can do." I said as I grabbed his outstretched hand and shook.

Once I did this though, two fires burst out of our palms. Mine spouting green flames, and black from Xaraxis's. The green flame quickly crept up my arm, not burning in the least, but consuming our bodies at the same rate. "Don't be afraid." I heard Xaraxis say, but to this, I merely looked down at the fire moving to my chest and down my legs, and said I wasn't in the least.

The green flames slowed as they crept up my neck and covered my head. The same had happened to Xaraxis only the color was changed to black. The flames replaced our bodies and began to meld together, starting from the arms and slowly moving in, until the two of us became the same flame. A mix of green and black hues. We were the same flame. The same body. The same person.

*   *   *   *   *

The next thing I saw was the familiar wall of my room. The room I was given when I first began my journey as a Guardian. I had no idea how long I had been asleep, but it couldn't have been a new day. The clock next to my bed reassured me by showing that it was only eight-o'clock. With how unbelievable the past events had been, my mind almost made me believe it was only a simple fever dream. A simple dream gone haywire from an overexertion of energy. Only… some part of me. No, not just some part, but all of me wanted the events to be true. I wanted it to be real. All of it.

All of the pain I had felt when I passed out had left my body, and I got out of bed with ease. Yet still, I slowly strode out of the doorway and into the common area of the bunker. I noticed Ruby sulking in the doorway to the kitchen, and Cinder was still typing away at her computer, acting as if she was already over me, or that she knew I would pull through. I was hoping for the second choice.

The fear that had earlier eclipsed all of Ruby had faded, and she was left with a look of soft melancholy. "I just can't believe I could be so stupid. He was my responsibility, and I blew it."

Cinder ceased her typing and looked back at her, annoyed. "Ruby, for the last time, this was not your fault, it could have happened to anyone, and he is going to be fine! Now quit moping already."

I walked in, not saying anything. Ruby's eyes grew bigger than they had ever before. "You're okay! All this time I thought Serpente had killed you." She said, almost hyperventilating as she ran out of the room. I assumed to get Jack and Ryder.

I sat down in an empty chair and breathed a sigh of relief. Perhaps now, I could finally find out what everyone was hiding from me.

"It's good to see that nobody did anything drastic. That just shows how optimistic everyone truly was." I heard a familiar voice say. I looked at the couch next to me in time to see Xaraxis appear.

"Ahh," I shrieked in surprise. "What are you doing here?"

Xaraxis laughed at my barely masculine action. "You've already forgotten our deal, haven't you? I exist on your plane of perception until you relinquish control, and once that happens, you will exist on this plane until we once again trade off."

"So, what you're saying is... you're like my familiar." I asked, smirking.

Xaraxis made a face of both amusement and annoyance. "If you want to call it that, go ahead kid. Technically speaking, I'm merely a double personality anyways."

Cinder looked up from her laptop and glared at me with concern. "Umm... Ronen... Who are you talking to?" She asked, seeming quite concerned.

I looked back at Xaraxis sitting right next to her. He shrugged, not knowing what to say. "You mean you can't see him?" I asked. Cinder raised an eyebrow and shook her head. "Huh, strange," I said in reply.

Cinder continued to stare at me. "I think that serum did more than just make you pass out." She then went back to her work, leaving me completely confused.

Xaraxis burst out laughing the very moment this happened. "Ha, now she thinks you're schizophrenic." He continued to laugh for a solid minute, before speaking again. "Like I said. I only exist on your plane of perception. See." He said as he moved his arm behind Cinder. I waited as he made a motion as if he were going to slap her, but rather than making contact, his hand completely went through her head. "I guess if you really think about it, it's a lot like schizophrenia. However, once we trade off, I gain control of your body and you end up in my place. It's just like I said before."

As Xaraxis finished his demonstration, Ruby walked back into the room accompanied by Ryder and Jack. Both of which seemed to be surprised to see me with a full recovery. "I must say, when you said he was awake I had my doubts, but this is simply unprecedented." Ryder said in shock. He turned to face me. "What do you remember of Serpente. What happened before he drugged you?"

I looked over at Xaraxis who was now standing at my side. He slowly nodded his head up and down. "Tell them... then show them." He said reassuring me to tell everything.

"As you already know, Maxwell Serpente ambushed me out in the training field. He drugged and took me to his facility where you all rescued me. What happened though, was that I met one of his disciples. A boy about my age, named Hunter. He possessed the power to change the gravitational force of certain objects. He was a person who seemed adamant on rising through the ranks and joining his high council. He was welcoming at the time, but I don't think that will be the case anymore."

"He probably grew up under Serpente's rein. All he knows is the Serpent Corps." Cinder said, seeming to pay the most attention. In the corner of my eye, I could see Jack holding a solemn face, as if he had known what I was going to say.

"Most likely." I continued. "Anyways, I was later dragged to a research lab by a woman named Mickala Morris. She was very closed off and I think she had some mental power because I noticed a blue gloss go over her eyes just like Ruby's when she touches a weapon. She strapped me to a table and left. That's when Serpente came in and drugged me, saying he could lead me to the truth. That I was embracing ignorance. It was just after that when I was rescued by Jack."

Ryder nodded as I told the story. "You met one of the kids and Mickala Morris? Interesting."

"What does she do though?" I asked him, trying to get an answer to my own answer.

Ryder nodded again and spoke. "It's pretty simple. She's a scryer. Mickala Morris can see through the different paths of time, allowing hindsight on what can happen in future events. The thing is... she can't tell which path will be taken, so it isn't as useful as it could be. Is that everything?" He asked, seeming more interested than before.

"In terms of Serpente, yes. But there's a lot more. When I passed out, I was met by an alter ego of myself. Get this though, he was the beast. That uncontrollable being I couldn't seem to gain any control of. Eventually we came to an agreement that when needed, he would get control of my body and in return, use his power to protect us. To my surprise though, that made it so that he exists on my… field of perception, for lack of better words." I said. Everyone else looked at each other with the same look Cinder had given me earlier. "I'm telling you, he's real. I can show you."

Xaraxis smiled and nodded once more. "It's time, grab my hand, this comes easy." He said, holding out his hand again without saying anything. I grabbed it without a second thought. Strangely, his hand seemed solid even though I had just seen it pass through Cinder. Not to mention the fact that the others were merely seeing me grabbing the air. I held my grip as Xaraxis pulled my arm. Immediately, I felt as if my soul had lost its physical being as the two of us merged like in my dream. Seamlessly though, we separated, and Xaraxis entered my body, leaving me only in his view.

My body slowly changed, leaving black scars down my right eye and past the arms, changing from my body to Xaraxis's. He raised his head, looked down at his hands and smiled. "Greetings Guardians. Don't be alarmed for I don't come with malice intent. I am Ronen's transformation. The one you called beast, demon, and more recently uncontrollable being." He spoke in a tone deeper than mine. It was actually quite strange to hear someone else's voice coming out of your body. "My name is Xaraxis by the way. I have seen everything through Ronen's eyes. I know all of you, and it obviously goes without saying that I want to help you destroy Maxwell Serpente. In fact, I as well believe that I am the key."

Ryder stood up and shook his hand. "It's very good to see that Ronen's finally figured out his power. Hopefully now we can begin to formulate a plan for the downfall of the Serpent Corps." He said, very hopeful.

"You actually believe this. How do you know this isn't just Ronen speaking in a deeper tone?" Said a girl leaning against the doorframe to the kitchen. She must have had walked in when I had transformed. I recognized her as the girl who rescued me back at the Serpent Corps facility.

Xaraxis frowned with an annoyed look in his eyes, "If the obvious burns on my body don't show it…" he started, creating a single axe in his open hand. Even I was surprised to see that unlike my green axes, the color of these were as black as the darkest of midnights. He then proceeded to twist his body and hurl the axe into the wall with maximum strength. "That should be enough."

The axe disappeared, and he turned back. Everyone stayed still, eyes wide. Another man entered the room and looked straight at the girl in the doorway. "Wow, he certainly proved you wrong. How does that feel?" He was the other man I had seen before, distinctively.

The girl looked back at him and sneered smugly. "Shut up Parker." She then stepped out of the doorway and sat in the last empty chair opposite of where I was sitting. "So, your name is Xaraxis? Nice to meet you I guess."

"As am I with all of you," Xaraxis said with a smile. "But as it pains me to say, Ronen's body can only hold out for short amounts of time even if I'm stationary. I really should switch back with him."

Ryder nodded in understanding. "I see. If that must be, go ahead. After all, you'll still see and hear us on the other side.

"That is true," Xaraxis said while looking at the other six people. "Goodbye everyone." He said holding a hand out to me. I grabbed it and repeated the process that had happened before, returning my soul to its rightful place.

I opened my eyes once again to see my fellow Guardians staring straight at me, except for Jack who was looking back at the hole in the wall made by Xaraxis. "Incredible. Simply incredible." He said with his mouth agape. "In all my years I have never seen a power with such strength. I mean this guy just threw an axe into solid metal. You may even rival Serpente himself… if not one of the original Guardians."

I nodded, accepting what he had said. "I guess, but it does have its drawback," I said holding my hand against my chest. "Just that short amount of time puts a lot of strain on my physical body. Maybe even my mental state." I stopped for a moment to survey the other people. The concern had fled from their faces and were replaced by surprise. "What can Serpente do anyways? He never said anything about his abilities when I was with him." I looked over at the couple who were sitting adjacent to me. "And who are those two?"

Ryder took over for Jack in answering my question. "The two over there are Agents Parker and Brittany Steel, partners from the Texas branch of the American Guardians. They've actually been married for… about two years now?" He said, turning to the two of them for confirmation.

They both nodded, and Ryder continued. "Parker can increase his muscle mass to use as shielding or to add power to an attack, and Brittany distorts light, allowing herself to become transparent in lighter areas, and pretty much invisible if dark enough." He stopped, allowing time for the information to register before finishing his statement. "Ronen… these are the unwavering gauntlets of the Guardian Agents." I looked over at the two of them. they were holding hands at the time and waved as if to introduce themselves.

Jack regained his speech once I looked back. "They're one of the first agents I met outside of the Serpent Corps; and one of the most powerful too. But it still took both of them working as hard as they could to even make a scratch on Serpente."

"Why is that?" I asked, cutting him off.

Ruby was the one to answer rather than Jack. "You know how I once told you that powerful versions of the Guardian gene can create multiple powers along with the original? Like how you have those axes and your transformation to Xaraxis?" I nodded back in total understanding, while looking to where Xaraxis was. To my surprise though, he was just… gone. I disregarded it for a moment though, knowing he would be back.

Ruby continued. "Well… from what we have observed… Including his original, Serpente possesses four separate abilities."

I widened my eyes out of awe, wondering how powerful that actually would make him. Logically speaking, that meant he was at least twice as powerful as I was. "What are they? He never showed any power while I was with him."

Ruby shook her head steadily for a single moment. "That may be true, but you did see something when he kidnapped you this morning, but I will get to that eventually." I suddenly realized that all of this had only spanned one day. It was definitely the most eventful day I had lived in my entire life.

Ruby continued. "First, you need to know who Serpente is." She then looked at Ryder sitting on the arm of the couch.

"Ronen, if I were to ask you who my first student was, who would you answer with." He asked.

I looked around to the people in the room with me. "Ruby. For like twelve years it was just the two of you until Cinder was found seven years ago. Then two or three years later, Jack joined your team, and three weeks ago, I was recruited. The newest of the team."

After I finished talking, Cinder made a sound like a game show buzzer, saying I wasn't even close to the desired answer. Ryder shook his head slowly. "She's right. You left out one person."

I once again looked at the people in the room. "Who's left? The only other people here are Parker and Brittany… and they're both Texans."

Ryder began again. "It's not them... this happened before them. long before them. this happened... oh, about two-hundred years ago, after I uncovered the amulet which is now in Serpente's possession. However, inside the tomb, there was also the writings of who I assumed to be from Aaron of Cairo, the original Guardian himself. A prophecy of events to come, and some of what has already happened. Cryptic depictions of battles with odds completely against us, and one person able to wield the amulet to rise above. However, it also said that if this person was corrupted, all hope would be lost."

I continued to listen to every word he spoke. "So, what's your point? It's obvious that I'm not corrupted."

Ryder sighed. "That wasn't my point. Because of that prophecy, I let my own fear and haste get the better of me, and I put all my trust into the first person I saw with the Guardian gene. In my haste though, I let my guard down and told every one of my secrets to my original student... Maxwell Serpente."

Ryder stopped for a moment to let what he said sink in. I couldn't believe what he had told me. The absolute leader of the Serpent Corps couldn't have been a student to Ryder. It just made no sense.

Ryder continued. "He worshipped the idea of being the earth's savior. Even after the amulet rejected him. So much that he began to become obsessed, resenting me. His corruption followed, and he left me in favor of himself. His true dream now is to prove this to everyone. Prove that he is the strongest of all the Guardians, by defeating all of us so that the Serpent Corps have nothing to hold them back. They could do anything without consequences, including enslaving all of humanity, becoming… some type of god for them.

I stood in awe for a moment. "So, if that happened two centuries ago, Serpente must also be able to reverse the aging process. Just like you can."

"In a way." Ryder continued, assuming a role which reminded me of an old village elder telling stories to children. "The Guardian gene did gift me the power to reverse my biological clock at will. Over the years I figured it was so that I could be a good teacher. What personality trait that relates to is beyond me."

I looked to Cinder just in time to see her mouth one word. It was hard to make out, but I still knew exactly what she said. It was the same word I had pondered on in the past.

Integrity.

Ryder continued. "I do implore your perceptiveness, but Serpente does not have this ability. Though some might work in similar ways, no two powers are completely identical. Like me, Serpente can reverse the aging process. But unlike me, he can only achieve this through the use of a catalyst. Serpente's main ability is to leech the life away from others for his own gain, but only to keep himself young, but also like me, he can't instantly heal wounds received in battle. He can stay alive forever, but he needs to kill for it."

"If that's his power, what makes him such a formidable opponent?" I asked, in slight shock to what I heard. What kind of person would have the audacity to savagely attack people to stay alive?

To this, Ryder ushered towards Ruby. She looked around the room as if too seem surprised and spoke again. "His main power isn't a problem for us, especially since he can't leech off other Guardians. But like I said before, Serpente possesses four separate abilities." Ruby then held up a finger. "One: as Ryder said, Serpente leeches the life energy from non-Guardians to keep himself alive." She raised a second finger. "Two: like you observed when Serpente kidnapped and drugged you, his second ability is to synthesize any chemical from certain ingredients." Ruby then added a third finger. "Three: Like his second power, Serpente also has a strong immunity to any kind of poison. Believe me, we have tried to kill him three times like this." Finally, Ruby flipped a fourth finger. "Four: Serpente can use the life force he absorbs to shield himself from attacks. This is his most powerful move and can only be summoned a select number of times before his body gives out, or he runs out of reserves, but in that time, he can defeat any challenger. It is this power that makes Serpente such a formidable opponent. We all have encountered him at least once and know that he is the main source of corruption in the Guardians." She lowered her hand before continuing. "There is absolutely no saving him. The only way to truly save anyone… is to completely destroy Maxwell Serpente and everything he stands for."

Her last words were something I already knew. Maxwell Serpente was already too corrupt to be saved. The only way there was to save him was really to kill him. That realization however would not make the job any easier. If it were me, he'd be the first life I ever took. But if it was for the good of others... if it was to save them, I'd have to come to terms with myself, and do it. "Well, I guess that only leaves one more question. What do we do now?" I asked. "How are we supposed to get rid of Serpente?"

Everyone looked away to try and think of an answer. It was eventually Cinder though, who was the first to speak. "I know an informant who lives around the city. I bet he knows the internal layout of at least the training facility pretty well. If we leave tomorrow morning, we can be back by noon."

Ryder nodded in assurance. "Then we can formulate a plan on how to infiltrate the facility again."

Ruby stopped Cinder before she could speak again. "If you can though, don't leave until around ten. If we really are going up against Serpente himself again, there is one more thing I must teach Ronen."

Cinder nodded. "Sounds good. We can still make contact, but we might not be back until dark. So... looks like you're going to have to put your trust in two teenagers."

I couldn't help but laugh at Cinder's retort. Ryder just rolled his eyes. "Then it's settled. Rest up everyone, because tomorrow, we have work to do." He said as he stood up and walked out of the room with Parker and Brittany. I assumed it was to show them a room. Cinder and I left as well, leaving only Jack and Ruby sitting at the table.

*　　　　*　　　　*　　　　*　　　　*

One minute after Ronen and Cinder left, Jack stood up to leave, knowing what Ruby was about to ask him.

"Jack. She was there, wasn't she? She was in the facility?" Her voice was soft and supple, yet strong, looking for an answer.

Jack sighed and sat down again. "Yeah. Talia was there," He said in a consoling voice. "She hasn't changed at all. Still thinks of me as a traitor. She also wanted me to give you a message. She said she's ready for you, and that she will be victorious in the end."

Ruby nodded with a frown. "I thought it would be something like that, but it can't happen. Talia's power may be special, coming from her natural flexibility in both body and mind, but she can still be overconfident. She can be as much of a threat as possible, but I still can prevail."

"If it was three years ago, I'd agree with you." Jack said with another sigh.

"What are you implying?"

Jack continued to stay silent until he found a way to say what he wanted. "I have reason to believe that Talia has recently unlocked her U.A. I didn't see it, but she seemed more confident than the last time I saw her. I know this must be tough for you, but I knew you would want to know."

Ruby nodded once more and folded her hands in front of her. "I did. In fact, … I'm glad. It just makes her a more formidable opponent. I expected it; she is my sister of course."

117

"So then," Jack started. "If you do end up having to fight her, what are you going to do?"

Ruby once again became silent, only speaking when she knew for a fact what to say. "I'll do what needs to be done, and hopefully that means I can save her." She then got up and took a few steps to the doorway, then turned back. "She isn't completely corrupted. There are ways to save her from Serpente's lies." She then turned back and left, leaving Jack alone. The last to leave. He sighed again and said one more thing before turning out the lights and leaving. A sentence he truly believed.

"She can be saved… just like I was."

10

"I am not a bad person. By all means I certainly don't enjoy getting angry with my disciples." Serpente said, seething with rage. "But that doesn't mean you all are off the hook." He banged his fist on his desk beginning to yell. "Not only did you allow our prisoner to escape, but you also let that snake Jack infiltrate this utopia and walk off with him."

Inside with him was Ms. Mickala Morris (another high council member and Maxwell Serpente's trusted assistant). The young Hunter Haines stood on the other side of Serpente's desk. His chakram in hand, having just come from practice. Talia stood next to him, holding in the rage for the man who had paralyzed her hours before. She was still twitching a bit from the electricity.

The next disciple in the room wore all black including his hair complete with gray eyes that could peer through a person's soul. A light scar was etched into his face from the outside of his left eye to the top of his cheek. He was the third of the Oregon Serpent corps, also known as the Elite Serpents, Xavier Manuel, the lead of the research division, with the power to control animal populations with only a thought and a whistle.

The last of those inside of Serpente's office was a very small girl, her sleek ash brown hair pushed back in a ponytail. This girl was Ivy Storm, the youngest of all the disciples. It was Serpente himself who found her when she was only six. Her power unlocked after watching her father abuse her mother. Like her name suggested, Ivy had the ability to sporadically grow and bend plant life to her own desire. She was finally discovered only after slaying her father with this very power.

"I'm not happy with any of you... and knowing that our secrets may have been leaked doesn't help in the slightest," Serpente said, continuing to sneer at everyone in the room, then looked back at Mickala standing behind him. "How many timelines have you looked through past Ronen's escape?"

Mickala stopped for a moment, parasitized by fear. "It's hard to really tell. Maybe... a couple hundred. Or a thousand."

"And in how many do the Guardians return to destroy us?"

Once again, Mickala paused. "About six hundred. But they have intent to kill you in all of them.

Serpente nodded. "Then we must be ready for it. Talia, I'm putting you on the front line, meaning round the clock patrol of the perimeter. If you see as much as a bird perched on a tree, do not hesitate to slay it.

Talia nodded and left the room. "As you command," She said as she left.

"Hunter, I'm stationing you in the library. You will serve as our last defense in case our facility is breached. Do not hesitate to attack, but make sure to take Ronen alive," Serpente Commanded. Hunter smiled, nodded and left without saying a word. Serpente continued. "Xavier, how far are you in your research of the Ferals? Have you finished training them?"

Xavier spoke with his normal, deep voice. "There is still work to be done, but they have shown substantial improvement over the last couple of weeks."

"Guard them in the labyrinth and seal all other entrances. I give you permission to use them if necessary."

"I will personally make sure they are ready." Xavier then left, silently. Leaving only three.

"What's my job, Sir?" Ivy said in her soft, high pitched voice.

Serpente looked at Ivy strait in the eyes. "This is only because we need everyone on our side. Act to guard the inner sanctum of this building. Don't feel restricted though, use one room, or block off all of them if you wish."

Ivy smiled brightly. "Thank you, Master Serpente." She said as she turned to make her exit. Leaving only Serpente and Mickala Morris in the room. Alone, together.

Serpente sighed. "All the time I spent to build up this garden of mine, finally in danger of destruction."

He looked back at Mickala, holding her clipboard of daily jobs. She seemed calm, yet she was shaking inside. "Of the six hundred timelines that you viewed. How many do we succeed?" Mickala Morris opened her mouth to talk but was immediately cut off. "No, I've changed my mind. In how many… do they die?"

Mickala's eyes grew wide at his request "Are you sure?"

Serpente turned back to his desk and stared into a mirror. He looked inside it back at Mickala, "Positive. I need to know"

Mickala looked away for only a moment, then spoke. "I don't know… maybe about thirty or so."

Serpente smiled. "Good." He stood up and walked over to her. "Let me ask you. What truly makes a garden? Is it the flowers… or those who plant them?" his face turned somber, pushing the anger from him. "You don't know what it's like, building a garden of Eden, and then having it all go to hell. I tell you it's just torturous." He ran his hand down her cheek, feeling her soft, supple skin. "But they will be destroyed, I know it. You aren't like the others here… you know that? Everyone else may be strong, but they're also arrogant. Only you, only your ability brings humility, but more importantly, obedience. That's one of the reasons why I like you so much." He let go of her and sat back down at his desk. "You may go now. Finish your work and then return here. There are some things you must know before the Guardians return."

Mickala Morris let out a sigh of relief and nodded, a small smile on her face. "As you wish… Maxwell." She walked past his desk and out the door.

"Oh, and Mickala." Serpente said before she closed the door.

"Yes?" Mickala said, stepping back into the room.

"…Bring me one of the powerless guards. One of the younger ones. Incase everything fails… I'll need to be at my full strength."

Mickala nodded with a blank look on her face. "As you wish." She then closed the door and left, leaving Serpente alone once more.

"My ability proceeds me, and once I'm done with these weeds, I will enjoy using them in my army." He looked back at his mirror and laughed. "Look at me, getting all worked up for nothing. There is nothing to be afraid of." He pushed a strand of hair to the side of his face, put down the mirror, and smiled. "If you wish to attack do so… but expect hellfire in the process. Game on Ronen Haven… Game on."

*   *   *   *   *

"It's hard to believe Serpente is already back. At this point we have to prepare as much as possible. I just hope today's lesson will be enough for us to win," Ruby said as she led me down the path to the training course. She had told me that above all, there was still one more lesson left for her to teach me. Yet it didn't seem like there could possibly be anything left.

I looked over at Xaraxis who had been walking parallel to me. "Well, now that you can give me control, why not try giving me a shot at a fight with her, maybe even knock her down a peg or two," he said while elbowing me in the arm.

I couldn't help but snicker at his comment. "As much as I want to see that happen, it's probably not the right time. Maybe after we defeat Serpente," I whispered to him. He laughed back and continued on. I noticed that at that point, he disappeared once more. Probably retreating into my mind like he did before I made the agreement with him. Nevertheless, I returned to Ruby and continued to walk through the grassy plain. "You know, at this point Ruby, the only thing you have above me is experience. If I trained for fifteen years, I bet I could beat you."

Ruby smirked and looked back at me. "I seriously doubt that, but you can dream." Even with the threat of Serpente on our heels, she didn't seem to be any more afraid than when I first met her.

Ruby walked up to the wooden training floor, then stopped me. "Before we begin, I want to brief you on what's to come. I cannot make this any clearer. Normally I wouldn't be doing this for at least another month or two, but with the new threat, I don't really have a choice."

"That's understandable," I said. "So, what is it?"

Ruby walked into the studio and continued to talk. "As you already know, the Guardian gene roots itself in the host's personality. It's these traits in fact that result in a Guardian's powers.

I stood in confusion, everything she had told me was what I had already known. "Yeah, what's your point?"

"I was getting to that. What you don't know is this, the gene roots itself deeper than the personalities. Along with your way of acting, your hopes, desires, and even your dreams are used. While the main power is rooted in the personality, there is a much stronger power which is formed through the grave scars that accompany you in life. From those memories, the gene can manifest into the Guardian's most powerful ability. The name for it is U.A, short for Ultimate Ability or Ultimate Attack depending on how the power is used. At least, that's the name we have for it. There's some scientific name for it that no one outside of the researchers bother to memorize it."

"So, when you told me that Serpente's most powerful ability was to create a shield from his condensed life force, you meant that?" Ruby nodded silently to my question, and immediately my eyes were full of wonder. "So how do I use mine?"

Ruby shook her head with a slight smirk. "It's not that simple. Just like the original abilities, the ultimate ability must be unlocked separately. I was pretty lucky to have unlocked my ultimate almost directly after my original ability, but even I have problems activating it sometimes. Even if I do, I get a splitting headache once it deactivates."

It seemed strange. Part of me wanted to find out what would come out of my desires, but the backlash could still be too much to bear. I already felt a certain weakness from transforming into Xaraxis, meaning the use of my ultimate attack could potentially cause me to fully pass out.

Ruby once again flashed a smile at me. "Perhaps you could use a demonstration. Let me show you." She then walked into the middle of the studio and raised her chin. "When I say go, create one of your axes and throw it at me. The harder the better." She said after cracking her neck and shaking her hands.

I stood in total disbelief. "You're kidding right?" I said in a perplexed tone. She stood less than ten feet away from me. If I threw an axe at her she would obviously get hurt.

Ruby smirked. "I'm dead serious. Come on, if you do, I promise you'll see something you won't expect."

I rolled my eyes and phased an axe in my hand. "It's your funeral." I said while drawing back my arm to aim.

Ruby didn't take her eyes off me throughout the entire time I was aiming. I noticed that right before she told me to attack, she closed her eyes, lowered her head, and muttered something under her breath. It was completely unnoticeable to anyone not looking straight at her lips and, even though I saw it, I couldn't figure out what she said. Once her lips froze again, she looked back up in confidence. "Go," She said softly.

I thrusted my forearm and body towards her, releasing the projectile at full force. The axe spun at a speed I had never thrown before, but Ruby didn't seem at all phased. Once it came close enough to her, she lifted her arm and stretched to the left. The axe continued to spin past her until it hit the ground, dissipating into shards.

I stood in slight awe as she smirked. I phased another axe, this time throwing it lower, aiming for her waist. Only to this, Ruby tumbled her body into in an Arial style backflip. Once again, my axe flew to the ground and disappeared into translucent shards.

I threw a third axe to her chest, only to see her once again evade the axe and grab it out of the air with her free hand. She once again smirked, walked up to me and held it out. "You want this back?" She boldly asked me.

I simply stood there until the axe dissipated in her hand. Then, mouth agape, I finally spoke. "How in Hell's name did you just do that?"

Ruby nearly burst out laughing at my question. "You really don't know? What you just saw was my U.A. at work."

She had managed to dodge every one of my attacks in a mere split second. It was incredible. If the strength of Ruby's gene, which was on the relatively weaker side, could produce such a power, what would that mean for Ryder? Or Serpente? Or even me?

Ruby continued. "I call the move Believe in Destiny. Once it's activated, I gain a sort of pseudo-time sense. I can detect incoming attacks as a form of numbness in the part of my body that would be hit. It really comes in handy against sneak attacks and any other surprises."

"I'm guessing you came up with the name?" I said still slightly in awe of what I had seen.

Ruby nodded slightly giggling. "Yeah. I know it's a little cliché, maybe even a little silly. It does mean a lot to me though." She sighed, "before I lost my mom, she said she would see me again, with my sister. She was always one to believe in true destiny, just as I do. The name is also pretty easy to remember. Once I say those words, it triggers the memory of my mother speaking to me. Those memories are what will trigger the ability. You could even say that memory is where my hope is rooted."

Ruby had told me that her mother was killed, and her sister Talia taken by a Serpent Corps member. It must have been then that her U.A triggered along with the awakening of the Guardian gene.

It was then that Ruby began to hold her hand to her head and stumble. I held a look of concern as she found her balance again. "That's the only downside to using an ultimate ability. The power heavily strains your energy supply. Once the ability deactivates, all that energy is taken straight from your body. I possess a weak version of the Guardian gene, so the downsides are low. However, for someone like Serpente, he runs the risk of passing out pretty much whenever his ability is overused. Be careful of that, because you possess a power stronger than most of the other's I've ever seen.

I continued to ponder about how this applied to me. I looked to my right to see Xaraxis again, sitting in the grass. "My taking control of your body already puts enough strain on you to push me back into the chambers of your mind. For all you know, the U.A. could send both of us back there. It would probably be best to avoid using it unless it's absolutely necessary."

I nodded back at him and turned to Ruby. "It truly is a powerful gift, but it always takes its toll. Remember that." She said solemnly.

I looked back and began to shrug. "I haven't even found out anything about my own U.A. and you are already warning me about the side effects? Shouldn't those steps be reversed?"

Ruby smirked once more. "Would you rather me have told you about it after you used it, passed out, and became hysterical upon awakening, unable to process any thought of it?" She said folding her arms.

"Point taken." I continued to focus on my own U.A. possibilities. When it came to my own desires, I never wanted anything too extravagant. Before my awakening as a Guardian, I never wanted anything more than to be successful. Graduate college, get a job, and live my life. However, at this point, I didn't want anything more than to complete this so-called prophecy and gain control of my life again.

I watched as Ruby almost obviously looked away. She proceeded to change her expression to a straight face. Although she had a slight curve in the right corner of her mouth. I spun around completely to see Cinder walking down the path, heading to us. Ruby looked to her wrist to check the time and began nodding. "Yep, ten o clock exactly." She looked back to our pursuer. "Punctual as ever Cinder."

Cinder glared back at Ruby, giving off a 'mother-daughter' vibe. "Can you blame me for wanting to keep things moving smoothly. It's not like I'm calculating to the second though." She then looked at me and reverted back to her casual self. "We can go ahead and head out if you two are finished with your lesson."

"He's good to go. I just had to brief him on the idea of ultimates."

Cinder looked back at me. "Good to know. You don't know how lucky you are to learn that so early. I couldn't use mine for at least a year after I even unlocked it. Anyways... are you ready to go?"

"Yeah, let's get this done." I said not trying to hide my excitement.

I walked over to join Cinder when Ruby grabbed my arm. "Wait," she said abruptly as she pulled me into a hug. She continued to embrace, not saying anything. She finally spoke after fifteen seconds. "Despite everything I said to you just now, there are times when you have to use your ultimate ability. For all you know, it might be when you first unlock it, but you will know when the time is right. When that happens, use it. It might just save your life." She then released me from her grasp. "Now go."

I walked over to Cinder, and we both left. Though I didn't see it, I knew both her and Ruby were smiling at me. Pleased at how much I had been taught from them, and how far I had come. They were truly part of my family.

11

I was surprised to see Cinder lead me all the way across town in a matter of three hours. The buildings were all decorated for the upcoming Christmas season. Some stores placed mountains of gift boxes in their windows whereas the streets were decorated with statues of reindeer pulling an empty sleigh. Every lamp post and storefront were wrapped in ribbon and tinsel and multiple trees were decorated with multi-colored lights which would not be turned on for another couple of hours. It seemed strange though, but the buildings I had once seen nearly every day somehow seemed to be bathed in a separate sheen. Like I had been gone long enough for pretty much everything to change. Even with the small amount of snow powdering the ground it just seemed like I was in a completely different state.

A sharp chill just cold enough to run through my jacket brushed against my skin, making my body shiver slightly and uncontrollably. This plus the scenery made it impossible to not picture my home and everything I had left behind. Growing up, whenever winter had first struck the ground with snow I would always run outside and play without any coat until I had nearly gotten frostbite where my mom would bring me inside, place me in front of our fireplace and make up some hot chocolate for the both of us. Then she would sit with me until I regained feeling in my hands, and even longer than that sometimes. She would sit and watch Christmas specials with me for as long as I wanted. No matter how long it was.

No matter what year it was I never learned and the tradition continued and she would continue to stay with me for as long as I wanted despite her workload. It was acts like these which proved how much she truly cared for me. The memories continued to flood back and couldn't help but miss her. I knew that even in this time she would be staring out the window wishing that I as alright. I felt so bad for her. I had never wanted to worry her like this ever, yet that was what I was doing.

I looked to my side to see a mirror reflection of myself. He held the same solemn look on his face that I did. He had probably heard my thoughts and was feeling the exact same way. After all, in a way, he was like my brother, meaning that she was also his mother.

Xaraxis laid a hand on my shoulder consolingly, still holding the same flicker of hope and mischief in his eyes like he always did. "I wouldn't worry much about her. She's strong, but more than that... she knows that you're just as strong as her. I bet she's at home right now awaiting your safe return, knowing that you're still alive."

I looked back at him and shook my head. "But that means she's still worried for me. For both of us, even if she doesn't know you."

"You can't think about that right now," Xaraxis began to say. "We both have a job to do and until it's complete we can't go back. You just need to let her worry for a little longer, and then that'll be it."

I nodded in understanding. "I guess you're right about that. We have a job to do."

Cinder suddenly stopped her trotting and turned back to me. "Is something wrong?" She asked with a friendly tone of voice.

I noticed Xaraxis lift his hand from my shoulder before saying one last thing. "You'll see her again. Don't worry about this. Just focus on the job at hand and trust that she'll be okay."

I looked back at Cinder who was probably now realizing who I was talking to. "Yeah, I'm fine."

"Well… okay I guess." Cinder replied before turning around and resuming her stride. I knew he was right, so without saying anything, Xaraxis disappeared from my field of view and I ran to join my guide once more. Continuing to walk through the well decorated Oregon streets.

Cinder soon led me to a side of the town I almost never went to. Down streets I didn't even know existed, nor had a need to visit. Eventually though, she led me to a place I certainly knew about, but never had the money, nor the seniority to enter.

In 1962, a relatively smaller size horse track was erected and quickly became the center for fun and fair gambling. The track became a symbol for the entire community. So much that when the owner died in 1996, the inheritors decided to build a statue in his honor in front of the building. However, by the time the drug crisis hit in the late 2000s, scandals began to pop up left and right. Cocaine and heroin dealings often happened under the table nearly every day, and it wasn't uncommon to see someone overdose as they watched their horse lose the race. It was because of this that my mother had forbidden me from entering. Even when the owners claimed to have cleaned the place up, the ban stayed. Frankly, I couldn't blame her.

"Seriously Cinder, your informant is in there? Is there any way you can get him to come out here to talk?"

Cinder shook her head as she draped her chestnut colored hair over her shoulder. "No can do. He'd never leave his post early. My informant believes that leaving his post causes him to lose 'millions in winnings'."

"How is that even possible?" I said skeptically.

Cinder stood motionless and smiled. "You'll understand when you meet him." She said with handing me an entry ticket with her outstretched hand.

Immediately upon entering, my impression of the facility changed from a drug den to that of a completely respectable business. Everything was almost shiny. The horses uniformly raced on the track as spectators ran through the hallways placing bets or simply passing through to get to their seats. Even the bar Cinder led me into was almost immaculate.

Cinder walked over and sat at the bar. I was pretty sure it violated some law since she was only nineteen, but nevertheless, I disregarded it and did the same.

Sitting next to Cinder though, was a large burly man with dark blonde hair. He turned to face her with a gruff smile. "Cinder, you never fail me. Not that I didn't already know you would show up. I even saw it clear as day." The man said in a deep voice.

Cinder smiled as she looked straight into his cool green eyes. "And you certainly haven't changed at all since I last saw you. Hard to believe it's only been three years. Have you considered rejoining the force at all?"

The man shook his head for several moments. "Serpente already believes that I'm dead, and I wish to keep it that way. I have a family, and I don't want them to be targeted." He stopped for several moments to think. "Now why is it that you suddenly felt the need to contact me after all this time?"

Cinder leaned back to reveal me sitting next to her. "The reason involves him, our newest member Ronen." She turned back to me, "This is one of the previously retired members of our team, Joel Cartwright. He worked as an undercover agent, joining the ranks of the Serpent Corps in order to feed us information on Serpente himself."

"So, what's his power?" I asked wondering how the man managed to trick Maxwell Serpente, especially in getting past Mickala Morris.

"Well-," she began but was suddenly cut off by Joel.

"Talk is cheap Cinder. In my mind, a demonstration is in order." He said while tapping the monitor of one of the betting machines. He manipulated the screen to view the ninth race and placed a bet. A slip popped out the bottom of the machine and the words 'thank you playing' flashed on the screen. Joel proceeded to set down the slip face down next to him before once again facing Cinder and I. "We'll look back at that later. In the meantime," He looked directly at me. "So, what is it that makes you so... special?"

His voice seemed stern, eager to get the topic off himself. I couldn't help understanding though, if I had to work undercover with Serpente for years, I'd watch my back every second too, even if he believed I was dead.

"I hope words are enough for you, because if I use my power, it will not be inconspicuous." Joel nodded, slightly irritated yet still keeping his passive tone. I leaned in slightly and spoke in a soft voice. "I transform into a demon at the touch of a hand." I was clearly overcompensating, but it seemed to work as Joel's look of intrigue finally showed. I looked past him to see Xaraxis, his arms folded, yet still smiling.

Joel continued to look interested yet still hid a certain face full of questions. "And how old are you exactly?"

His question was not one I had expected. With everything that had been presented in only a minute, it seemed peculiar that my age would be the first thing in question. "…Fifteen…"

Joel abandoned his passive, monotone posture and began to scowl. "Figures. He's got the power to match one of the elite Guardians, and he's a kid. I swear Ryder gravitates to you precocious types. What a letdown." He seemed to be overly disappointed at my age alone.

"And what exactly does that have to do with my ability?" I said, slightly offended.

Cinder held up her hand to Joel before he could speak again. "I can handle this," She said, and turned to me. "You see Ronen, the Guardian gene can naturally awaken itself when the possessor is around the age of twenty-five. Though, like all of the current Guardians on our team with the possible exception of Ryder, the power also can awaken from an intense amount of adversity or mental trauma."

I thought back at all the profiles of the Guardians I had met. There was Ruby who, at the age of sixteen, witnessed her mother, Rosary Leyva, die and her baby sister be abducted by a Serpent Corps commander.

Next was Jack Falsey, the master of static, who gained his ability from Serpente's sadistic experimenting at the age of twelve.

Even I who only three and a half weeks before had my ability activated after breaking into an anxiety attack, was underage upon awakening.

However, Cinder had never told of how she gained her ability. In fact, she hadn't disclosed anything of her past life to me, and maybe not anyone else besides Ryder who was the one to find her. With that in mind, her past must have been something so bad she didn't want anyone to know about it.

"So, I'm younger than most of the other Guardians. I still don't get why that's the problem."

Joel continued to form a scowl, constantly looking at the TV screen, waiting for his race to start. "For starters, Guardians reaching the age of adolescence upon awakening don't go through the multiple physical and mental changes associated with growing up. Essentially, the personality that is presented then, is the one that stays. In your case though, the premature activation leaves you immature, and while your personality might change, your power won't. Not to mention you can't go anywhere with age restrictions. It essentially makes the power a gigantic coping mechanism." By this time, the race was set to begin in only ninety seconds.

I looked over at Cinder brushing her fingers through her hair. "He thinks there's a difference between the two groups, but there really isn't." She turned back to Joel. "And what about me, after all, I awakened my powers when I was only ten."

Joel rolled his eyes and turned back to the screen in the bar. "I stand by my reasoning."

"Well then..." Cinder said, turning away from him. I looked at the screen in between the two of them, watching the horses being loaded. Cinder quickly turned back to watch. "I had a feeling this is how he would show you."

With the sound of a gunshot, the race began. Everyone in the bar sat in complete silence, watching to see the outcome. Not a sound was uttered for the ninety seconds the race lasted for. But as they rounded the last bend, everyone was surprised to see the winners. The Horse order was in fact number sixteen, number seven, number two, and finally number twelve who was apparently the favorite.

"I don't get it. How can watching a horse race demonstrate your ability?" The idea was simple, yet obviously had a hidden meaning to it.

Joel smiled for the first time since I had met him. He seemed very proud of himself as he picked up the betting slip and handed it to me. "Take a look at this. It should clear things up a little bit."

I turned the slip around revealing its contents. Joel had bet on a superfecta meaning the first four horses in the correct order he specified. I looked at the bottom of the slip to see the exact horses he had bet on. In first place, number sixteen. In second, number seven. In third, number two. Finally, in fourth, number twelve.

Joel had actually done it. He had guessed the superfecta of the race. A feat with odds greater than one in seventeen thousand, and based on his own expression, this was not the first time he had done this.

I looked at both Cinder and Joel. "Incredible, simply unbelievable. How is this even possible?" I said in complete and utter shock.

Cinder began to smile a split second later, then fully burst out laughing. "I can never get tired of seeing that face. Everyone he shows it to makes it."

She continued to laugh while Joel took over. "What she's trying to say is, my power is simply to see into the future."

I continued to look confused. "How can there be another scryer. Isn't that Mickala Morris's power?"

Cinder stopped laughing for a moment and grabbed the betting slip from my hand. "That isn't entirely true. While both incorporate the aspect of time, the implications are essentially the opposite." She then flipped the betting slip over and began drawing multiple lines protruding from a single point. "This is Mickala Morris's power. She sees through multiple futures as far as she wishes. The downside being that she has no knowledge of which future will come true." She then put a perpendicular line through one of the many branching paths. "Now this, is Joel's power. Unlike Mickala, he sees the future as it will happen. The downside to this though, is he only can see through a limited window of time."

Joel spoke up to take her place. "It usually isn't more than an hour or two at most. Not exactly the best of powers but it can come in most handy when fighting someone. Think about it, use the power, and you instantly know every one of your opponent's attacks."

I once again stood surprised at yet another power I had learned. He was right, even if the power was limited, the ability of seeing time as it would happen could easily be more powerful than any power the Serpent Corps had. It was easily better than seeing nothing but a jumbled mess of possibilities.

"But let's get back to you," Joel began to say. "What do you mean by 'turn into a demon' exactly?"

I looked back at him and began once again. "I haven't quite ironed out all of the details, but I can try to explain. I have an alternate personality named Xaraxis who feeds off of all my negative emotions. Once I give him control of my body, his strength and agility increase allowing him to complete whatever task I give him. Along with that, both of us can create axes at my own will."

Joel nodded in understanding, yet still pursed his lips. "But what if you're the one who wants control? What if you want the power?"

"I don't think it really works like that." I answered again.

I looked past Joel again to see Xaraxis shaking his head consolingly. "Sorry kid you're out of luck, but you still have a shot at the ultimate."

Joel watched as I stared past him, he turned around and was surprised to see that no one was there, despite what I could see. Cinder caught his shoulder. "Don't worry, he isn't crazy or anything, he's just listening to that alter-ego he just mentioned." She said, breaking the silence. "Anyways Joel, there is one other reason we contacted you. We need information... on the Serpent Corps. Specifically Serpente's main facility outside of town."

Joel stopped still, probably reminiscing on some previous event. "I never forget the layout of places I go to, but why do you suddenly want to mess with Serpente?"

141

"He threw the first punch." Cinder said. She almost snarled as she listed off the multiple reasons for overthrowing Maxwell Serpente. Some of which included his grudge against me, or that I could be the key that they were waiting for. She also mentioned past grudges against the Guardians as a whole. In the end though, Joel was nodding in agreement.

"Over the years, I have not only known the layout of the Serpent Corps mansion, but also learned of his army. Now, that part might be void because I haven't seen them in three years, so I'll probably just stick with the layout. I can't talk of it now though, so here's what will happen. I will be at your bunker tomorrow morning to tell you everything you need to learn, but obviously I can't accompany you."

Cinder and I both nodded and smiled to him. "Understood." She said completing the agreement. "Thank you for your consideration Joel."

*   *   *   *   *

After nearly an hour of Cinder and Joel catching up with each other, and me getting to know him, we finally left the track and were away from large amounts of people.

"Well, he was certainly something." I said to Cinder when we were finally outside.

Cinder nodded in agreement, a wide smile on her face. "Yeah, Joel's personality is a bit of an acquired taste. He has good intensions though, and he's a valuable asset to our team. Same goes for his power." She then looked at the sun which had fallen below the line of buildings across the street to us. "Anyways, we've got some time to kill before we have to be back. Any ideas?"

I looked back at the clock on the entrance to the race track for the time. By then it was only around four in the afternoon, so we had a few hours before we had to start heading back. Yet nothing came to mind of how we could spend the time, other than looking through the stores in the shopping district, which really wasn't my favorite thing to do after the first hour or so.

"I got nothing," I said shaking my head. Based on how she acted in leading me throughout town though, I knew Cinder would easily be able to come up with something to pass the time. "What about you?"

Just like I had predicted, Cinder nodded after only taking a second to think. "I think I know something that could be fun then." She way of saying it seemed very cryptic, as if what she was suggesting would be a fun surprise.

I squinted my eyes in confusion. "What are you proposing?"

Cinder pulled my arm until I was forced to face the street. "Tell me Ronen, have you ever danced with a real woman?"

"What?" I said as my eyes grew to the size of saucers. She didn't seem flirtatious about it at all, but her way of explaining was very unusual. It was as if she wanted me to be surprised at what she was about to say. I looked back to the last homecoming dance which was the only real time I had taken a date to a party. I ended up having fun, but I seriously doubted that it had anything to do with Cinder's sudden idea."

Cinder continued. "There's a small, classy club down the street. It's a place for waltzing and other dances of the like." She stepped into the street with the grace and carefree nature of a teenager, which she still was being nineteen. "How would you like to share a dance with me?"

"I don't know. Do we have time?" I asked slightly intrigued.

Cinder shrugged. "Trust me, as long as we get back by midnight, we'll be okay. What do you say? It might just be our only chance to do this you know."

I pondered on what it would mean for me to dance with Cinder. I didn't have any kind of crush on her bright green eyes and flowing chestnut hair. But perhaps if I did take her up on her offer, she would finally begin to open up to me. "You know... why not, it seems fun." It seemed so unlike me to say such a thing. At that point it had probably been the newfound confidence from my earlier training. Either way, a part of me wanted to relax and have some fun, and by the looks of things, Cinder was the same way.

Cinder and I both walked in silence down the block, taking less than ten minutes to get to the dance studio. It seemed completely inconspicuous with the other buildings but seemed utterly intriguing. Cinder paid for two tickets like she did at the horse track, handed one to me, and entered. "How do you get so much money?" I asked, but she only smiled in intrigue.

"You'll soon realize that I'm simply full of surprises, but this is just thanks to the fact that I don't spend the allowance Ryder gives me."

Once inside the building, I realized how underdressed both of us really were. While Cinder and I were wearing street clothes, everyone else at least had on a blazar.

As if somehow seeing my discomfort, Cinder laid a hand on my shoulder consolingly. "Don't worry about what anyone else might think. Being fancy is optional," she said as she grabbed my hand and pulled me out onto the floor.

It really seems quite comical, but when I was eleven years old, I actually enrolled in a cotillion. Half due to my mother forcing me, and the other half to what I tell myself was my own interest. It was there that I learned dances such as the foxtrot, salsa, and even waltz. I never thought I would ever use it, but as it seemed, I was clearly wrong.

I gripped Cinder's hand and put the other around her waist. I then led her in dancing to the beat of the music that played, dancing in circles like the other couples around us. Throughout the entire time, I couldn't look away from the eyes of her smiling face. "You're good at this," she began to say. "I never expect most men to know how to dance. In fact, I've had to teach every man I've done this with. But you're different."

I smirked at her smiling face while spinning her. "Well, unlike others, I care about this kind of thing. Speak for yourself though. How'd you learn to dance?"

Cinder's eyes darted to the side as she spoke. "I've had years of practice."

"You could say the same about your power. After all, haven't you had it for over seven years?"

Cinder kept her eyes off me as she went on. "Yeah. I got my power when I was ten, but Ryder didn't find me until I was Twelve."

"What caused it to happen? What did you learn about your power before?" I took a gamble in asking, but I really felt that both our mutual trust and literal closeness would get her to open up at least a little.

While I pushed her down into a dip, she spoke again, albeit in a much softer tone. "Nothing really. The only thing I learned was what my power really was. I didn't learn what it meant or how to shut it off until Ryder found me."

I pursed my lips trying to understand what she was alluding to and opened them again while I pulled her in close. "So then, what was your life before? What caused you to get that power, and even that personality?"

Cinder turned her head away, only to quickly look back. I could tell she wanted to explain her story to me. "I... I didn't grow up well. From what you've seen, I never stop moving. There's always something that I'm working on..., but there's a reason for that." She stopped, becoming utterly silent for a moment, and sighed before resuming. "Ryder did find me when I was twelve, but where he found me... was a foster home. I grew up there, abandoned by my parents from a time I don't even remember, and the closest I could get to them were through my councilors." My face immediately changed from consoling to sorrow at her description. "I suppose my power did awaken as a sort of coping mechanism. After all, if you didn't move fast in a home like that, you didn't survive. My power is based for that need. The need of diligence for survival. In the blink of an eye, I was able to finish all of my chores and still have the time to get food, but I was still stuck there. I tried to find those who wanted me, but I was always sent back. No one wanted a twelve-year-old with ADHD."

I couldn't imagine the pain she must have felt, or even the pain she felt by simply retelling it to me, yet her tone was just as it was before. Just the idea of being abandoned, thinking there was no place for you would be too much for me, and I couldn't help but be utterly spellbound by her resilience. "By the time Ryder found me, I was a mess. I didn't believe any family would want me. But he cared. He took interest in me, knowing about my power, and adopted me. It was right after he took me out of that hell that the second form of my power appeared, and my mental agility became just as fast as my stamina had become."

I stopped our dance after hearing her speak so clear and easily. As a kid, I had also struggled with some abandonment issues, having to watch my mother cry over every lost relationship. Wanting to find another person like my father. But that didn't even come close to what happened to Cinder. She had nowhere to go, and no one to go to. If it weren't for Ryder being a father figure to her, there would be no telling how dark of a life she would be living.

"That's terrible." I said, unable to speak anything else.

Cinder slowly nodded. I could feel her breathing steadily as she spoke again. "I can say for sure that it was. I went through the first ten years of my life without anyone to talk to. I could try talking to my councilors, but when there are fifty kids living in the same building, there's never the time. I could never get a word in edgewise, and to this day I don't even know if they heard me."

I paused, unable to think of what to say. It was understandable that Cinder would want to keep such a thing secret. This past showed her as a sad, abandoned, helpless child. She was ignored by her legal Guardians who couldn't give her the time of day. No wonder she was so reserved. No wonder she barely wanted to speak with me when we first met. It must have been how she lived in the foster system. It made total sense.

Along with my realization, Cinder began to tell more. "The thing is though. I can't be mad at this. Yeah, it was total hell, but I got out of it. Ryder adopted me, and I've never been back. I want to eventually, but I don't think I'd be able to take it at this point. What I want to say though is that this event fueled my desire and changed my personality to what the Guardian gene wanted. A twisted past turned me into something beautiful."

"So... does that mean you disagree with what Joel believes?" I asked still looking in her eyes.

Cinder shook her head for the umpteenth time that night, only to continue talking. "All of it. In fact,

I believe the opposite. It's the adversity that we go through that makes the personality, and when those events happen to us, the result is what stays with you forever. That is the personality you stay with your entire life, and even if your ideals change, it does not. So really, the gene activates because there is no reason for it to wait. Even if we're not as mature as the others. It just gives us more time to practice… and get stronger."

"I'm guessing then that you have already unlocked your U.A then."

Cinder snickered in a way I assumed to be in confidence. "Of course. I unlocked it three years ago. It was the first time I was able to beat Ruby in a fight."

"What is it then?"

Cinder continued to smirk, bringing her lips to the corner of her face as she pulled me around to her hip. "Do you really think I would tell you all of my secrets in one night. You might get something like that from Ruby or Jack who are open books, but I take a little bit more finesse. I've told you my past, don't get greedy." She then laid a hand on my cheek. "Don't worry though, I'll soon reveal it all to you, but all in due time." She sounded very cryptic for that moment. No telling if it was intentional or not.

We continued to dance and converse with each other until the clock read 7 P.M. by then, it was both our decisions to leave and begin to head back to the bunker and deliver our intel. I couldn't help but feel closer to Cinder as we left the upscale dance studio. Not love and affection, but trust and respect, like she was an older sister, or best friend. For all I knew though, she was trying to be flirtatious. Even so, I couldn't focus on that, all I could think of was what she meant by revealing her secrets to me all in time. This probably meant that she had more to tell than just her U.A., perhaps even another sub-power other than her cognitive abilities and stamina.

"I really had fun tonight Ronen. I haven't danced like that in years." She said to me as we left.

I smiled at her, though slightly tired. "Same here. To be honest, I never knew you could have so much fun dancing."

"Well, that's probably because you haven't danced with me until now. What a way to go out with a bang."

I wanted to stop and ask what she meant by that, but I already knew. If we were to die in the siege, there would be nothing left. This night, me dancing with Cinder could be my last memory of celebration.

Only I didn't want that to happen. Above all else, I wanted to live to figure out as much as I could about my power. I wanted to find out all my inner abilities, both physical and mental.

"I wouldn't be scared though Ronen," Cinder began to say. "After all, this time we have a new weapon. A new variable to add to our defenses." She was trying to be reassuring, as if reading my inner monologue. "With you added to our defenses, Serpente will be defeated."

I continued to walk, ignoring her last comment. Part of me knew it wouldn't be as easy as Cinder had said it. Serpente had his own team just like us. They trained for years with the intent to kill each member of our team. They would continue to pursue us even after Serpente was dead. Even though Hunter Haines and Mickala Morris were the only ones I had seen, Serpente had to have at least double the forces. There was one thing I didn't understand though. One thing that still went without answer.

When Serpente had me restrained in his lab, he mentioned that I had just barely scratched the surface of my destiny. Obviously, he meant that I was oblivious to the existence of things like the ultimate ability and probably a multitude of other secrets. But then there was that black sludge he pumped into my veins. From what Ruby had told me the previous night, Serpente could create any chemical compound from normal everyday ingredients. It made sense that he would make something like that, but the effect was still strange. It was as if the drug made me lose control of my body. Eventually making me meet Xaraxis face to face. He said it would open my eyes, and in a way that's exactly what happened. Serpente gave me control of my power, probably as a sign of peace. I didn't buy it though. There was something about him that did nothing but make me wince. He seemed like the kind to strike fear into the eyes of everyone he saw. And by the way I saw Hunter, this seemed like the case.

Hunter seemed like he built himself off of the idea of humility. This could be the reason why he was able to control the pull of gravity on objects. While the proud harden hearts and stiffen others, the humble pull others closer, as if affecting their own pull. Meanwhile, Serpente posed as a man of a separate kind of integrity than that of Ryder. A kind of integrity that well compared to my mother's most recent boyfriend, Jerry who showed his caring nature by thrashing me outside of a police officer in a time where my own anger and fear let Xaraxis loose for a second time, and there were consequences that went along with it. I could only imagine what my mother could have done. Forget Jerry being right in all his accusations of me, that didn't excuse him from being a complete narcissist. And then there's my mother who had to stand up for me over the entire six months he lived with us. She always said I was a good person at heart no matter what I might have done. If he were to go off on a tangent of how he was right all along my mother would probably lose it. She had known all along about how much that man had tortured me. If that happened, that would be it. The final straw, and she would get rid of him for good.

Serpente acted exactly like this. He lashed out at me for a single attack... and that was only me being with him for a couple minutes. The rest of his miniature army had to live with him full time. There was no telling how many times he had lashed out at them. With this in mind, and the backstory Ryder had provided where Serpente was the secret fallen Guardian who lost his way out of sheer jealousy of others like him, there was only one trait that came to mind. The only possible trait that could create such a heinous power as leeching the life force of people to stay young. A trait that fit the personality almost to a tee.

Vainglory.

A state of pride that only considered pride in one's self. Serpente sought to prove that he was Stronger than any other Guardian. It was this that motivated him to create the Serpent Corps in the first place. Now his rival organization was probably stationed in multiple countries just like the Guardians were. Even if we destroyed Serpente, a new leader would be chosen from the existing members in its reticulation. Probably one of the lackeys in his round table. Someone like Mickala Morris or even Hunter considering how adamant he was when I spoke to him. The point being that there was more to his organization than just him. While his death would surely cripple the infrastructure, giving us a chance to strike a larger blow, it would not destroy the Serpent Corps, but that was an idea for another day, and possibly another branch of the Guardians. I really doubted that everything would be solely left to us. For what I assumed, after such a feat took place, I might have gotten the chance to meet some of the other country's' leaders in what I assumed to be the Guardians High council.

"Ahh. Get away from me!"

The sudden sound pushed me out of my train of thought and back to reality. There was no mistaking it, the scream came from Cinder. I immediately began running to the scream's origin and walked up to see a wolf growling at her. It slowly moved closer, yet Cinder was frozen in sheer fear.

In the far-off distance, I could see a shadowed figure resting on a close hill leaning up against a tree.

I listened closely to hear a faint sound of a disembodied whistle.

Immediately, my thoughts and memories fused together, revealing the identity of the hidden marauder. This was the same man who sent a family of wolves to attack me the day my power awakened. I quickly phased an axe and lobbed it at the shadowed figure.

I watched as the shadow man took a step out of the axe's trajectory. Cinder, who was no longer looking at the wolf stood dazed and confused at my actions, probably not seeing the shadow.

The figure slowly stepped forward, allowing his body and face to be illuminated by the moonlight. His gothic style haircut rivaled his black cloak. Under it though, I saw that he wore blue jeans and a white colored shirt. Only one eye shone on his face, a mix of the colors green and silver. "What are you doing here?" I said with great concern. To this, he let a grin fall on his face.

"I was wondering when you would see me Ronen, but now I must go to master Serpente and tell him my cover has been blown. Oh, how lamentable." The unnamed marauder let out yet another whistle to his companion. "Nevia, to me." The wolfen attacker growled at Cinder once more, then returned to its apparent master.

"Who are you?" I asked, marveling what I had just seen.

The marauder ran his hand over the coat of his wolf, named Nevia. "My name does not concern you. Nor do my reasons for being here." He let out another whistle, signaling the wolf to lay down in patience. "What I allow you to know is this, Serpente wishes you dead, and he will stop at no cost to see that happen. You may have just begun your time with those misfits, but it's all about to end."

Anger pooled in my body like floodgates being breeched. Without even thinking, I phased another axe, and bolted towards him. The still unnamed man began to form an O with his mouth to signal another command to his companion, but before any air left his lips, I restrained his body, holding my axe against his neck. "Whistle and your life comes to an end here and now."

The unnamed man laughed at my advance. "My my, I never pictured you to be so bold. Perhaps I've misjudged you."

I scowled at him, prepared to slit his throat at any moment. "You are toying with my last nerve. I seriously suggest you pick your words carefully." Anger continued to grow inside of me. so much that it surprised me that I wasn't switching with Xaraxis.

"Easy there Ronen. Don't do something you would regret in the future now." A voice said from behind me. In shock, I released the hand restraining the marauder and turned, still holding the emerald green axe to his neck. My gaze met yet another midnight assailant. This time, it was a young male with flashy brown hair, wearing a garish red jacket and blue jeans. The clear giveaway though, was the gray chakram hanging from his belt.

"What's stopping me Hunter?" I said, clenching my fist around the axe held to the other man's neck.

Hunter rolled his eyes, at the same time he reached into his pocket. "I don't think you would want to lose something this important for good." He said as he opened his fist and dangled a thin black necklace out of his hand. Hanging on the lace was a small metal cross with six bands. Four at the far end, and the other two intersecting in the middle. This thing in Hunter's hand, was the amulet that Maxwell Serpente had stolen from me two days earlier. "Kill him, and you will never see this thing again. I can promise you that."

My body froze at the sight of the lost amulet. Even though being without it forced me to make great strides, I needed it in the possession of the Guardians. As Xaraxis had said when I first met him, the amulet had more uses than to block out a dangerous power. I had no other choice. I released my grip on the axe and stepped away from the marauder. The axe shattered on the ground at his feet.

"Thank you for your cooperation." Hunter began to say as he held the necklace in his palm once again. "Sadly though, you've left yourself defenseless." Hunter then grabbed the gray chakram from his belt, and in the bat of an eye, hurled it at me. I quickly dashed forward, leaving its path as the circular blade cycled around the vicinity and then back to its thrower. "I hold all the cards. I have the high ground. Now you won't even get a chance to see Serpente again. Xavier, now."

The previously unnamed marauder, now freed from my grip, whistled to his companion. Immediately, the wolf Nevia stood and growled at me, ready to attack. Cinder was still frozen in shock, unable to move from the reveal of both Xavier and Hunter. "I'm sorry we have to be rid of you before tomorrow's fun, but we do have orders from Serpente himself." Hunter said as the wolf drew ever closer and eventually pounced, her sharp talons and fangs barred as she approached her target.

To avoid this, I quickly slid my shoe ninety degrees and rotated my body, only allowing the wolf to connect a single scratch. The attacker retaliated by once again charging, only this time I didn't avoid her attack. Instead, I intersected two freshly made axes and blocked the Wolf's swipes. It was then that I saw a weakness.

I noticed before that the wolf named Nevia previously walked with a simple limp while retreating to her master. Even with this though, she didn't stop attacking at a menacing pace. However, it was obvious that she wouldn't be able to keep up through worse pain. I released one of my axes from the intersection and thrusted it to her front leg. The axe embedded itself less than an inch into her leg, but it was just enough to draw blood. The wolf wretched and howled in pain, but still attempted to attack, leaving open a window for me to throw my other axe into her side. The axe dissipated, leaving a huge gash on the wolf who soon collapsed on the ground, unable to move.

Xavier screamed as his companion fell to the ground. The only expression that was recognizable was his shock. "You roach! Do you have any idea what you just did?" He looked back to his wolf still strewn on the ground, and then back at Hunter, his face seething with rage. "I only wanted Nevia to wound you, but you will pay for this. Hunter… destroy him."

Hunter smiled as Xavier went to pick up his wolf, barely moving on the ground and once again entered the shadows. Without saying anything, Hunter once more whirled his chakram in an obvious attack meant not to wound… but kill. With new axes in my hands, I blocked the weapon, sending it back to Hunter. He continued to attack in the same way for nearly a minute, hoping I would get tired and slow down, but it was to no avail. Hunter continued to throw, obviously increasing his own gravitational force. "Give up on it already," he began to say. "You know I'm stronger than you, and it's only a matter of time until you die." I felt my anger grow, but I couldn't give up my body just yet. If I did, that would be it. Hunter had me in a sort of corner, at I saw no way to get out of it.

By the time three minutes had passed, I felt my muscles burn from the constant movement. Though hunter never stopped, I could tell he was beginning to wear down too, but his anger still grew with every throw. "As I said, I'm stronger than you. with every throw you get slower, until the final hit slices your neck."

With what little breath I had left, I screamed out to hunter. "You're wrong!" In sheer rage and envy, I made my final decision, and yelled to the sky. "Xaraxis! Take my body and slay this enemy!" In that instant, my conscience left my body. I watched as the body that was once inhabited by me, now by Xaraxis opened his eyes. Immediately, black scars began to cascade down his arms and right eye.

"Sir, you have no idea what you've just awakened." Xaraxis said in a mellow tone. Still, Hunter seemed unphased as if he knew all this time what could happen when Xaraxis was awakened. Nevertheless, Xaraxis charged at him just as the wolf did minutes ago. An act fueled by full rage alone.

In a sharp roar, Xaraxis created two new axes, each a deep void black, and prepared to pounce on his pray. Still, Hunter kept a clear face as if he had already figured out a retaliation. All he did was raise a hand confidently. Xaraxis leapt into the air poised to attack, yet once he was a foot away from Hunter, he was stopped in midair and fell to the ground in restraint. "It seems that blind rage can't get you everything," Hunter said as he placed his other hand in front of him. Xaraxis seemed to be almost pinned to the ground. "I do want to make one thing clear; this is not out of rage towards you. In fact, I think of you as a worthy adversary. However, orders are orders, from a superior, and a friend." He began to laugh in a menacing tone. "Who cares if he said to leave you alive. Once master Serpente hears word of your death by my hands alone, he will finally realize that I am worthy, and I will rise through his ranks and join him and Mickala Morris on the high council, as an elite fighter of the Serpent Corps. Anyways, it was fun for the short time we were opponents. But sadly, it is at an end."

Hunter focused on his hands and slowly pushed down. I watched as Xaraxis wretched in pain. At the same time, I felt the same searing pain in my chest, as if my rib cage was breaking and the air in my lungs were being forced out of my body all at once. I fell on the ground, immobilized by pain.

Hunter looked down, consolingly. "I'm sorry it's not painless, but it will be quick. All I have to do is compress the air until the pressure crushes your ribs and eventually bursts your heart and lungs." He laughed for a moment before continuing. "It might seem impossible, I mean after all, air is the hardest form of matter to manipulate since it has no real gravitational force. It moves so quick and sporadic, but even it can be moved, to those with enough power. Just goes to show you what five years of training can do for a person, now I can manipulate practically anything," he monologued. My chest went numb as if my rib cage was cracking. I still couldn't move any part of my body.

"I'm sorry kid," Xaraxis said as he finally lost all power, returning me back to my body and sending him back to the deep recesses of my mind. My eyes began to bulge as the breath left my body. I felt all the life force begin to die from my body.

Then as if the night sky opened up to save me, I heard a voice scream out. "Vestige Inferno!" I could recognize it no matter what, the voice came from Cinder who had finally snapped out of her trance. I strained my neck as much as possible to see her. Cinder's shout had also caused Hunter to lose focus, giving me enough leeway to see, but to my own surprise, she wasn't where I had seen her frozen before. In her place was a trail of flame leading to the tree line. They were short lived and quickly faded to ash, only burning the grass in its narrow path.

"I refuse to watch you kill him without a fair fight," Cinder said from the complete opposite of me. "If you want to just destroy our one chance at victory, you have to destroy me first."

Slowly, I regained feeling in parts of my body. I craned my neck to see Cinder standing only a few yards from both me and Hunter. Unlike only seconds before though, this Cinder stood in utter confidence. Her chestnut colored hair danced behind her as if being blown by a gust of wind. Behind her was the same trail of fire leading up to the back of her feet. In her hands was a bow etched with a fine tipped arrow. Her stance was one of pure fierceness, ready to fight at any moment that warranted.

"Well would you look at that. Miss Ember finally managed to snap out of her trance. Just in time to save her friend. How hilarious is that," Hunter said, bursting out laughing. "Tell me though, what do you expect to do with that bow of yours. You probably couldn't even stand to hit the tree behind me."

Cinder held her ground, pulling back the string on her bow. "I've never missed a target in my life. now get away from my friend," she said from behind her bowstring.

Hunter smirked, not letting up. "Go ahead. It's fun to watch you try."

Cinder pulled the bow up to eye level, and without saying anything, released the arrow from her grasp. The crimson arrow whirred past my head, and past Hunter's shoulder, hitting the tree directly behind us. With a face of confusion, Hunter looked back at the tree and slowly shook his head. "Well, I suppose I was wrong about one thing." His sudden disposition left me with just enough time to phase a single axe which I swung into his leg.

Within seconds, he was on the ground, wretched in pain. "Bastard, you think you've won, but you have nothing. You are nothing but a cockroach to me," he yelled as he laid on the ground in pain.

Cinder put her bow back around her chest and slowly began to shake her head. "Who said I wasn't aiming for the tree." I looked back at her, watching her sharp scowl. I had never seen such a look on her. She kept this face until she met eyes with me, only to suddenly drop her head and turn. "Come on Ronen, Time for us to leave."

I looked at her beginning to walk away, then back at Hunter. I couldn't help but pity him, even if he had tried to kill me. It was only then that I realized what he still had around his neck. He placed the cross amulet around his neck before the fight without me even noticing. It had to have been the reason for how he was suddenly able to manipulate the air. The amulet amplified the user's power by an unknown amount depending on the way you used it. When I first received it, I used the amulet to block out my power until I further understood it. But If Hunter could cause such destruction with it, there was no way I could let him keep it. So, before I walked away, I grabbed the necklace off him and joined Cinder.

Before I was out of earshot, I heard Hunter yell one more thing to me. "You think you've won, but you're wrong! You will not defeat my master! I will be victorious in the end, just wait!"

I left him in the dark, unwilling to keep fighting. It was just best to wait until the siege the next day to take on Hunter for real.

Cinder walked a few steps ahead of me, unable to look back. I couldn't help but run ahead and find out what it was that made her so quiet. She had just saved my life after all. It was very unlike her to be quiet in a time like this. Something must have seriously been up.

As I slowly got closer, I heard her mumble something under her breath, intending for me to hear. "Ih swarah." I had no idea what she could have meant though.

"What was that?"

"Inm sworrow." Still an illiterate mumble.

"Speak up already."

"I said I'm sorry!" Cinder belted out, almost making me jump. "It's just... I don't know. Once I saw that wolf, my mind just locked up. I just couldn't move until I saw you about to die."

I understood what she said. In fact, it had happened to me the first night I awakened my power. Ironically, it was the reason I awakened my power. So much stress had come upon me that I forced Xaraxis to take over. It was a form of mental overload which I assumed only affected me. Apparently though, it had different effects on other people.

Dampening, inhibiting, or even rendering a power completely out of control.

"This has never happened to me before. I don't even know what it was," Cinder continued with a horrified look. "How am I supposed to go up alone against Serpente himself if I lock up while facing one of his lackies?"

I stopped her at that. "Who said you were alone? Cinder... there are five of us. You won't be alone. Even if you are the only one fighting the other four will support you. You're not going to be alone again." Cinder nodded, and finally started to smile again. "Good, now what the heck was that move you just pulled back there?"

Cinder's eyes split secondly darted away from me as she spoke. "Oh yeah, that. That was... my ultimate ability. Vestige Inferno is a move that matches my speed to my stamina. When active, I move so fast that a trail of fire follows me, burning the ground up to the backs of my feet. It's why I wear flame resistant shoes."

"Interesting. So, what you're saying is that your ability adds a whole other variable to battle. On top of formulating a strategy, you can also flee if needed." I then realized what I was saying. "Why didn't you do that back there?"

Cinder stopped her stride for a moment, allowing me to catch up. "Oh, I didn't mention that? It's actually a simple explanation. Any sort of bulk added to my body dramatically lowers my max speed. If I were to carry you with me, I wouldn't get away fast enough. So instead, I used it to get my bow and save you."

"Still, that power is both offense and defense. If you use it tomorrow, there is no chance of loss-." I started to say before Cinder cut me off.

"I wouldn't count on it. Whether I can use it or not depends on how much adrenaline my body is producing. If I use it without the proper amount, my stamina becomes shot until I get the proper rest."

There was truth to what she said. Adrenaline had the power to turn normal people into complete powerhouses in strength, agility, or even dexterity. According to Jack it was all the adrenaline being released into my bloodstream which supported my transformation into Xaraxis in the first place. Perhaps, the more adrenaline going through the bloodstream, the less of an effect the ultimate ability has after deactivation.

Every single turn made me respect Cinder even more. To think, a foster child with nothing could turn into someone like this. A complete powerhouse.

*   *   *   *   *

The two of us didn't speak much the entire trip back. Cinder seemed reserved, but I knew why at this point, and I understood. She stayed silent for almost the entire time. Frankly, despite all I wanted to talk about, I didn't mind the silence. It seemed necessary to have a bit of reflection after such an event, and the night before we were to return to the Serpent Corps facility no less. It all seemed like too much for anyone to handle.

It was near eleven when we finally returned to the bunker, our job completed along with a little knowledge of our opponents. Though something still flashed a red light in my mind. I had absolutely no idea what it was, but it continued to linger. I decided to put it aside and think of more pressing matters. As we climbed the hill to the bunker, I realized something though. The words that Hunter had said as Cinder and I left seemed peculiar. He did nothing but boast on how he was stronger than me and how he would win no matter what. This was nothing short of the opposite of humility. But what else could give him the ability of gravity manipulation.

There was one clue, one thing he said while trying to kill me. "This is not out of rage, in fact, I think of you as a worthy opponent. But orders are orders."

I snapped out of my thought when Cinder unlocked the door and entered. Past the staircase and out in the rec room was Ruby sitting on a couch with the face of a parent who just caught their kid violating curfew. "What did you do?" She asked with her piercing glare.

"What are you talking about, we just completed our mission," Cinder shot back in a voice to prevail over Ruby's.

Ruby continued to glare at the both of us. I soon felt like I was in a police interrogation room again. "Please, I know your 'I just did something stupid' look Cinder. So, tell me, what did you do?"

It was at that point when I broke and told her everything. About how Cinder took me dancing and how we were ambushed by Hunter and Xavier. She slowly shook her head while listening.

Ruby continued to stare us all down. "So... did you get the cross or not?" She asked, still holding her hand to her hip. I nodded and pulled the necklace out of my pocket.

Immediately, Ruby changed back her sweet yet fierce persona I had first met. "Good, and with that, the Serpent Corps have no chance. Now rest up, we head out as soon as we have the information from Joel. Cinder, we can talk about this another time."

I could see Cinder's mouth begin to widen, only to close altogether without a single word. Clearly, she knew that at this time she was being let off easy.

With those words, I headed to my room and went straight to bed. For once, I did not have any kind of fear for the next day. It was strange seeing that there was so much to be afraid of, yet I was so utterly calm. The same as my first night with the Guardians.

"Let's just hope we can surprise them tomorrow." Xaraxis said inside my thoughts. *"I think we might actually have a shot now."*

I didn't bother saying anything back. He knew exactly how I felt. We actually had a chance, and I intended to take it to its full extent. With a bit of luck, we could actually defeat Serpente, ending his reign of tyranny once and for all.

But there were still so many questions left to be answered. Like how Hunter knew where Cinder and I would be, or what part of his personality had manifested Hunter's power. Most importantly though, was what exactly the amulet, now in my possession, would do if I used it again. However, my brain was unable to answer these questions. So instead, I drifted off to sleep, waiting for the next day to begin.

12

To me, the night lasted only a couple of seconds. I was unable to dream with all the anticipation. It truly was hard to believe that all of this was even real. That I had awakened super powers that had laid dormant all my life. Gifted to me by one of my parents and very well the one final defense in this world. It was simply unbelievable to anyone who hadn't seen it in action.

The seven A.M alarm blared through my ears, awakening me from my light sleep. I stood out of bed allowing my own fierceness to show. I was ready, knowing that this day's attack would not be easy, and that there wasn't a certainty that we would succeed. None of us wanted to wait for another opportunity though. The day had finally come. Maxwell Serpente's last day. This was the day that the Guardians had waited for since Ryder lost his very first disciple. With confident steps, I walked into the rec room to meet the others in my team.

Ruby, Jack and Cinder all sat on the couch in the middle of the room. Ryder sat in the chair to their right, and to their left sat our informant, Joel Cartwright. They all looked at me in exasperation, watching as I walked past them and joined the group of three.

"Well, now that the rookie has joined us, I can begin explaining the plan," Joel began. He pulled a small poster size blueprint out from under his chair. He proceeded to unroll it onto the coffee table and began motioning around the perimeter of the two-dimensional building. "Due to Mickala Morris's power, it can be assumed that the Serpent corps already know of your coming attacks. Because of this, all of the above ground entrances will most likely be sealed. Even if they aren't, the outside entrances would be to most heavily guarded. Instead, I propose you all use the only underground entrance."

He then pointed to a single spot on the north side of the building. "Serpente has installed a series of tunnels under his facility. This is the place where he dumps the remains of the people he leeches off. Don't worry about them though. They've lost every true human ability. They can't speak and can hardly think. They only really shamble around looking for an exit, husks of their former selves. It is this labyrinth that you will have to traverse if you want the best shot at getting into Serpente's stronghold." He then pointed to another diagram of the inside facility. "From there you must traverse the halls, go through Serpente's arena like library, and face him in his study, which is where Serpente spends most hours of the day. From there, it's up to you to defeat him and any other enemies that stand in your path."

The plan seemed simple enough, and it would have been if it wasn't for the reinforcements Serpente had. I only knew of four of them, but he had to have extras. They would have a chance to let us pass, but they obviously wouldn't take it. It did mean that we didn't have to kill them though. We only had to find a way to stop them from fighting us. It would be a whole lot more difficult, especially since our two subordinates from the Texas branch left for home the previous day with their own work, but it would be worth it.

Our main focus wasn't even on who would be the one to finish Serpente. It was how to dispatch his battalion. The first, and perhaps easiest to disband was Talia Leyva, the younger sister to Ruby, possessing the ability of contortionism. She fought with intense speed, making it tough for anyone to hit her, no matter how powerful the attack was.

The next member was one of the two who had ambushed Cinder and I the previous night. He was Hunter Haines, A boy who believed to be my personal rival. It was clear that he wished nothing more than for me to be defeated by his own hands. Hunter could manipulate the forces of gravity on a single object, and when he wore my amulet, could even control the air itself in a form of pseudo-telekinesis.

After Hunter came the other member of the previous ambush team. In a way, he was the first Serpent Corps member I had encountered. The midnight marauder, Xavier. I didn't have the time to figure out his last name or even his intentions, but I did see his power. Xavier could take control of different animals, giving orders through a sharp, high pitched whistle. He had even tamed a wolf and appeared to treat her like his companion. It made me actually feel a little bad for what I had done to Nevia.

The final opponent other than Serpente himself was his own assistant, Mickala Morris who had the ability to view the multiple timelines that occurred through the natural flow of time. She probably had already predicted that we would attack them all. Just not how, since there was no way to see which timeline would come true. I had yet to see her in a fight, but in being the right hand to Serpente, she had to be unbelievably skilled.

These four would be some of the strongest opponents we had ever met, and this time we were on their turf. The five of us certainly had our work cut out for us, but we were up for the fight of our lives. All of this wasn't even including Serpente himself.

"I will not lie to you. this will not be easy. Knowing Serpente, he will have traps and surprises around every corner, not to mention the other lackies he has, but with all five of you, you've got a fighting chance. It's not impossible, trust me." Joel concluded, rolling up his blueprint in the process.

"Well, I believe I speak for everyone when I say we are believers… even when the chances are astronomical. Every part of us will certainly be used," Jack said while the others pondered on Joel's description of the building's layout. His assumption was right though. Even the trans-mundane entity named Xaraxis believed that the core of success relied on the usage of everything you had. Even if it meant passing out later.

"Obviously," Cinder addressed to everyone. "This is our one moment. The moment we've been trying to get for all these years. It's better to finish the mission before some perfect storm begins anyways."

Everyone, including Joel, nodded in agreement. This was our one chance before another problem began. If we waited any longer, there was no telling what plan Serpente would formulate. We couldn't just wait for a perfect storm to rip apart everything we had built. We had no reason to wait.

"Perfect, because you will need to give your all in this if you even want a chance, but I have faith that you will succeed," Joel concluded, standing up from his seat and walking to the hallway leading to the surface. "I want to wish you the best of luck. I hope to see you all again, after Serpente is gone. Goodbye, Guardians." He then left the room, walking to the surface, and away from all of us

Everyone else sat in silence, waiting for someone else to speak. We were all confident, but that still didn't stop the anxiety from creeping up on us. There still a chance we would lose, even if no one wanted to acknowledge it. One wrong move and that would be it. Serpente would win, and there would be nothing left.

"So… what now?" Ruby asked, breaking the deafening silence.

All of us looked at each other, easily showing how uncomfortable we were. There was no shame either. Even I knew it. There was no sugar coating it, our mission was to kill someone. It's not something to shy away from, even if the job was for the greater good of everyone. In the end though, it was Ryder who spoke again.

"Unless anyone has anything else to say, I guess we head out."

Everyone said their answer one at a time.

"Nope."

"Not that I know of."

"Everything I wanted to know has already been said."

Their responses were almost identical, including mine which was only a simple shake of the head.

"Well... I do," Ryder said with a melancholy expression. "I don't know which of us will face Serpente in the end, but I can say this, it is nearly impossible to fight him head on alone. You might recall that Agents Parker and Brittany were pretty much the only ones to take on Serpente and land an actual attack. This isn't simply because they are both incredible forces, but also because they took advantage of Serpente's only know weakness." He paused for a moment to allow this to sink in. it seemed inconceivable. Serpente didn't seem to have any weaknesses other than his strong sense of pride in himself, let alone allow someone to know about it.

"You see, one of their best traits is that both Parker and Brittany fight in tandem of each other in nearly every case. That's where most of their potential lies.

The thing is, this is also one of Serpente's weaknesses. By splitting his attention between the two of them, Parker and Brittany managed to vitiate Serpente's unstoppable power, giving them an opportunity to act. It is because of this that I will not under-stress this. The easiest way to defeat Maxwell Serpente is to fight with someone else. Only then do you have a chance, but otherwise, don't fight him head on."

He didn't act like it was very important, but in reality, it was anything but. This was the one weakness we knew of. For all we knew, it could be the final nail in the coffin for him. In fact, some part of me knew that this would be his downfall.

"You act as if it's not important Ryder, "Jack said with a wide-eyed face.

Ryder quickly shook his head without looking at anyone. "No… no not at all. In fact, this might be the most important thing I have said of him so far. It's just… huh, I can't believe that we're about to kill my first disciple. My prodigy."

Ruby walked over and gently put a hand on Ryder's shoulder. "None of us blame you for this. I know I certainly don't. After all, it would be hard for any of us to kill you if the time was needed. But you, I, and everyone else know that there is no other way. Serpente is beyond saving at this point. If we wait any longer, he'll only get stronger until there isn't a chance for us to beat him. You need to simply face facts. The time to attack, is now."

Ryder slowly pushed her hand off of him, and picked up his head, the same expression on his face. "Your right. This must happen now, lest we face a new challenge before ridding ourselves of this one." He stood and walked past us, heading to the exit. "I guess this that means it's time. Our transportation is outside," He said while ushering the four of us to him. We all at once stood and followed him out of the room. In my head I could hear Xaraxis chattering to me.

"Good luck kid. I can help out as much as I can, but at the end of the day, it's up to you to slay the dragon and finish the quest. It's time for the reign of the Serpent Corps... to end."

With his words repeating in the back of my head, I walked out of the bunker and began the trek to the final battle against Maxwell Serpente and his infamous battalion.

*   *   *   *   *

The helicopter loaned to us by the Guardians Texas branch touched down on the outskirts of the Serpent Corps mansion within an hour. The building was distinguished in a fashion to look like a simple hillside mansion. Only the inside was definitely something else. It was actually the first time I had seen the building from the outside. I would have when I was first kidnapped, but I was infested by the serum Serpente had injected me with.

"This is where it all comes to an end," Jack said, returning to the slightly menacing person I had known before. "Which way are we going, Ryder?"

The simple black-haired man pondered for a minute before answering. "The entrance to the labyrinth is on the north side of the building."

At that moment, the five of us were on the eastern entrance, all we needed to do was move along the right of the building. But while moving along the tree-line, we noticed one thing out of place. Positioned next to the labyrinth entrance was a small girl, looking to be maybe twenty at the most, with hair the color of tree bark and a figure strangely similar to that of Ruby. She also had claws attached to her gloves. Upon closer examination though, I realized that she was the same girl I had seen paralyzed on the ground while escaping the Serpent Corps only days before. This was the girl who stimulated Ruby into unlocking her power. The girl taken from her when she was only sixteen. Her long-lost sister, Talia.

As Jack noticed the girl waiting in front of the building, he seemed to tense up. "Approach with absolute caution," he said as he took a few steps forward, all the while rustling the leaves beneath his feet. Then, almost as if on cue, Talia stopped where she stood and peered at the direction, we were standing in. I could just see her face as she twisted it into a sadistic smile. We all stopped still, hoping she didn't notice us when…

"I know you're there. I know you're all there." She stood, still staring at us. "The charade is over, so just come out!" She yelled, prompting all of us to walk out of the tree line in tandem of Jack. It was then that Talia began laughing. The kind of laugh you would expect from a total sadist. "This is it? This is all you brought? You expect to take over the most powerful member of the Serpent Corps with only five people. You've got to be kidding me, I bet you can't even beat me."

"What makes you say that?" I yelled back to her.

Talia continued to show an incredibly snide face. "Simple. You all are some of the weakest Guardians I have ever seen, especially that has-been I have for a sister. Sure, in an ambush you can immobilize us and run, but you won't kill me. no Guardian I've ever met could." She continued laughing at our expense. "It's actually quite comical, you do all your fancy talk about saving, but it never works. Here you all stand before me, trying to be assassins. You're not fooling anyone though. You five are so confident, blinded to what you are about to face. Once you enter, this becomes a gladiator match. You enter as gladiators, and you die as gladiators. You are not ready for what's in store, and since you've come for a fight, you'll get one. Jawlat wahidat tabda. [Round one, commence]"

I was slightly caught off guard by her words. Especially the last sentence. She had said something in a language I didn't even understand, nor did I even know what language she was speaking in the first place. Nevertheless, Talia brandished her claws and charged at me, prime for attack. She attacked in a series of overhead slashes, matching my every movement as I tried to retreat.

For the split second I was out of her range I tried to create an axe, but fell short when she would lunge, closing the gap. Every time I tried to phase one, she was right on top of me, leaving me no other choice than to dodge her attacks and hope for an opening.

Talia knew what she was doing too. By using close range attacks, she could effectively prevent anyone else from attacking for fear of hitting me. If Cinder tried to shoot an arrow at her, she would run the risk of me getting in the way, whereas Jack's widespread attacks would hit both of us. It wasn't even possible for me to release Xaraxis or create an axe, effectively making every possible attack useless. Even if I waited for overflow to occur, she would simply stab me mid transformation. That only left two possible challengers with valid attacks.

"You can try to dodge but you're just too slow," she said while charging in close and kicking me. I stumbled back in disorientation before she spoke again "It's a shame I only got to do this once, you seem like a fun sparring partner." Talia sneered and prepared to thrust down on me, pushing down with full force.

swcree, the sound of metal hitting metal assaulted my ears as two swords crossed the path of Talia's claws. I looked to see the owners to be Ruby on the left, and to the right, was Ryder. Their combined strength had managed to effectively block Talia in a stand still.

Ruby cocked her neck to the side, facing me. "Ronen get out of the way. I can handle this!"

"I can help. Just give me a second to make an axe."

Ruby shook he head, straining to keep her sword up. "This is my problem and mine to finish alone." She stared back, almost not caring about the attacker. "Just believe."

In that moment I understood what she was saying and stood to retreat as fast as I could to where Jack and Cinder stood. They both stood ready to attack. Jack arched static between his hands, whereas Cinder was simply holding her bow. I finally created a pair of axes and took a throwing stance. Ryder also did the same, leaving only the two sisters.

Talia smiled with what seemed to be joy at Ruby who stood in attack. "I never thought you'd have the guts to fight me sis. After all, we're the only family we have. What's the point of squandering it away? Join me and we can fight of these marauders as sisters."

Ruby released her sword, freeing Talia's claws. "I don't need your twisted love. I have a family and I won't let you kill them."

"As do I," Talia retorted. "and I'm not too keen on letting you just murder my master."

It was in that moment that I realized how similar Ruby and Talia really were. Though they had opposite morals and almost sixteen years in between them, they still wanted to protect their friends, despite their malignant ways. It was actually quite respectable.

Talia was the first to attack leaving Ruby to fall to the defensive. In a single movement, Ruby parried with an upward slash and then proceeded to attack using her unarmed left hand, and based by her form while punching, it was easy to assume that her power extended to martial arts as well as weapons.

Talia stumbled back in surprise at Ruby's sudden counter. As she regained balance, she sneered and commenced another attack crossing both arms. Ruby, unable to parry multiple attacks in such a short window of time was forced to block, sustaining a set of scratches down one arm. However, in the time that it took Talia to recover from the attack, Ruby lunged back, opening a window for another attack.

"Ronen, Cinder. You know what to do!" She yelled, stepping further out of the way.

At that moment, Cinder and I looked back at each other, then at our respective weapons before realizing what she meant. The two of us had talked about forming a duel attack using the ranged variant of my axes and Cinders bow, but we never actually took the time to see of it would work. Nevertheless, we had no other choice if it would end the fight in a single move. Cinder pulled back her bowstring while I lifted the jade throwing axes above my head. Then, I immediately hurled the two projectiles at our attacker.

At that moment, Talia recognized my axes flying past her and pulled into a backbend which turned into a full flip. However, what she failed to realize while taunting my bad aim was the second projectile hitting her in the middle of her ribcage. The impact was only meant to lull the target into a sense of shock, but in Talia's case, she was fully knocked out.

"No one ever notices the second attack." Cinder said while shaking her head, almost pitying her. She turned to me with an impressed look on her face. "That was good though, considering we've only talked about it." I nodded in agreement, unable to voice and opinion to the idea I had originally thought of as absurd.

Ruby knelt down at Talia's body and held her neck to feel her pulse. She looked over at Cinder with a very concerned look on her face. "That wasn't a fatal shot... was it?

Cinder quickly held her hands in defense. "No. No. Definitely not. These arrows aren't meant to kill. All they do is release a sleep toxin once the puncture the skin, I swear. In fact, I'm actually surprised she took the hit so hard."

Ruby slowly relaxed once she found Talia's pulse. She placed two fingers on her lips, then placed them on Talia's. All while saying something under her breath. "See you again soon... little sis." She stood up, acting as if nothing had ever happened. She walked away from Talia's body and towards the Serpent Corps mansion, turning back when she realized that none of us were following her. "Come on, if we don't move now, we'll miss our chance."

All of us shrugged off her dramatic emotion shift and then followed Ruby through the open entrance into the Serpent Corps labyrinth.

Upon entering, the first thing I saw was near complete darkness. The only sources were dimly lit blue LED lights meant to illuminate the entire hallway. Every corner showed two paths, one to the right, the other to the left, and throughout every turn, the halls were littered with the so-called husks. The many victims of Maxwell Serpente's leech power. They didn't even look at us though. They were completely drained of all life. Their eyes were just glazed over with nothingness. No thought was going through their minds.

"It's like they're not even alive," Ruby began to say, waving her hand in front of one of the shambling husks. "All they're doing is walking through the halls, devoid of thought, not even blinking."

Jack looked another husk strait in the eyes and frowned. "This is the last stage of his power. He can't destroy the body, so instead they're just left down here to die. If you ask me, It's one of his most despicable acts."

In truth, he was correct. In the next turn there was another husk, slumped over, entirely lifeless. I watched as within seconds, nearly a dozen living husks swarmed the dead body. They pulled off its limbs, swallowing the skin and various organs, leaving only a pile of bones soaked in a pool of blood. I couldn't help feeling at least some amount of nausea to the horrific display. Staring down at the empty skeleton and the husks feasting on the flesh of their brother left me fighting with all my will to keep my stomach settled. The same was true for my companions. All five of us stood in disgust and disbelief as the body was picked completely clean.

"How awful. Reduced to cannibalism. How low can someone sink? How can he possibly condone this?" Cinder muttered under her breath, still staring at the pile of bones. "This is what it comes to. There's just nothing left for them!" She pulled a short dagger off her belt and stepped towards another husk, ready to attack the defenseless entity.

"Cinder! What are you doing?" I yelled, pulling her back before she could swing.

"Well what am I supposed to do? There's nothing left for them! They're just abandoned! This is just the humane thing to do!"

"So, you'd just kill every last one of them? You think that's humane? If anything, you'd only be helping Serpente! And you'd allow him the perfect chance to flee!"

In that moment, I noticed a smell other than the rotted human corpse. A delicate smell of spring water mixed with something animalistic permeated my nostrils. A smell I had only encountered once before. I immediately pulled Cinder back in the same time that I heard a high-pitched whistle come through the hallway, followed by a shadowed marauder dressed in a black cape.

He spoke with his hair draped past one eye. "Would you look at that. Seems that an infestation managed to get past Talia's defenses. Tell me you 'guardians', do you know what happens when a fruit fly infests a pristine garden?" He asked, standing in the shadows. Without giving anyone a chance to think of an answer, another whistle came from the black marauder, prompting the same cannibalistic husks to suddenly turn and attack, grabbing Cinder and Jack, leaving Ruby and Ryder to struggle against the incomparable strength of the lifeless entities. "The answer... their exterminated," he finally answered. "What do you think? They're tough to train, but it's completely worth it."

Jack struggled to break loose from the grip of the husk… but was unable to loosen its grip. "What even are these things?"

Xavier smirked at Jack's attempt, but still answered. "They don't exactly have a true name. In fact, Serpente only opened the project a couple months ago. Although, I like to call them Ferals. So inhuman that they're practically animal, and once I train them to follow my every command, their power is simply unmatched." He turned to stare at me. "I would have brought my wolf with me, but sadly, Nevia is still in the care of our doctors. Thank you for that by the way."

So that's your plan isn't it? leave the dirty work to your friends and then finish the job yourself. You're such a coward!" I yelled to him.

Xavier did nothing but laugh. "Don't think that far into it, because you aren't even close." He said while ruffling the ends of his cloak. "As you can see, you are the only one who I haven't restrained. Instead, I propose a duel between the two of us. The winner will move on. Do we have a deal?"

I had no choice. If I wanted to move forward and take on Serpente, I would have to beat Xavier at his own game. On his own terms. "Deal."

Xavier smiled as he pulled a small pistol off his belt. It seemed strange though, but that was the only gun I had seen a Serpent Corps member with. "Excellent. Prepare for the fight of your life young Ronen. So, go ahead-." He aimed his gun strait at my chest. "Stand, bow, and target lock."

The second boss of the Serpent Corps cocked the hammer of the gun back at the same time as I pulled a pair of axes in front of my face to block. With the hammer pulled back though, Xavier made no trouble in aiming. Even when he pulled the trigger, I felt confident, but in an instant, the bullet flew into my axes, shattering both into a multitude of shards. I didn't want to believe it. Up to that point, I thought that my axes couldn't be broken. But watching the green shards lay on the floor, I couldn't help but feel useless. My muscles tensed up. No matter how hard I tried to will myself, I couldn't get my body to move. I just stood stunned, staring at the floor where the fragments had turned to dust.

"Oh, interesting. It seems that they do shatter. It just takes a certain amount of force." Xavier said as he put the pistol back on his belt and pulled out a more menacingly sharp rapier. "Naturally I can't actually fire a shot at you. That would just be beyond dishonorable. However, this will still be over quickly."

I still stood stunned. I couldn't move as Xavier advanced with his sword drawn. He squinted as he held the tip under my chin. "Oh, come on. So, I shattered your weapon. It's just not fun if you just give up now. Seriously, give me a challenge already," he said with the same monotone emotion. After nearly ten seconds though, he finally gave up and raised his sword. "Suit yourself then. I guess I was wrong about you."

Everyone behind me screamed in an attempt to snap me out of my trance. With every second they got louder. Xavier still rolled his eyes and thrusted the sword down on my neck. I braced for the impact.

"Damn it Ronen. You are not going to die yet!"

When the slender sword was inches from my neck, an axe clad in black appeared and parried Xavier's finishing move, I was again absolutely stunned by the weapon. I hadn't given control to Xaraxis and yet I was using his axe. Either way, my sense was regained, and Xavier was caught off guard. I threw the black clad axe at his body and dashed out of his way. I replaced Xaraxis's axes with my own, colored in a translucent jade, and prepared for my next attack.

"How dare you!" I yelled to Xavier as he regained his balance. "You aren't going to be the one to kill me! Not one of you will!"

"My, look who regaled the fire in his soul. Seems that we'll have a fight after all." Xavier sneered, ready to advance.

In a tremendous feat, Xavier and I continued to trade blows, but only seldom did either of us land a hit. Swipe after swipe he blocked and tried to pierce my defenses, only each time he did, I overlapped my axes to block. It was then that I realized he was slowly backing me into a corner and looking back I saw all my friends struggling to be released from the grip of the Ferals, but still to no avail. I had no choice but to give in even though my adrenaline had worked on overdrive to block out my fear.

"Xaraxis!" I yelled out, giving control of my body. Immediately my skin changed, leaving black streaks down the arms and right eye. The axes I held were also enveloped in a deep black.

"Big mistake." I heard him say as he pulled one axe behind his head and the other in front of him. In one swift movement he spun his core, ready to hit his target in an elegant bravura of an attack. The axes spun as he got closer, pushing Xavier's rapier out of his hand and using the other to strike, stopping only before hitting his neck. "Game over, animal guy," Xaraxis said before pulling back both axes and thrusting to Xavier's shoulder.

"Stop!" Xavier yelled when the axe barely could touch the hair on his neck. "You've beat me already." His breathing was more than steady, but heavy enough to cripple a bridge.

Xaraxis was thrust out of my body with his shout. I once again stood dazed, coming back to reality. "What? You aren't trying to kill me?" I was confused and still adhered on the side of caution. For all I knew once I let down my guard he would attack, even though that would still seem to be dishonorable to him.

Xavier's muscles relaxed as my axes shattered in front of him. "Make no mistake, I was. Only there isn't a need to fight any more. You win. You get to move on." He let out yet another high-pitched whistle, signaling the Ferals to release the other Guardians.

"Why though? What changed?"

Xavier took a single step back and continued to speak. "Contrary to popular belief, many of us don't wish to give up our lives. I realize that seems hypocritical, and to be honest, I only chose to fight you to judge your skills."

"Why does that matter?" I asked, finally letting down my guard.

Xavier pushed the tuft of hair past his face, revealing his right eye for a moment. "Every time I got a new opponent, I tested with the hope…. that they would someday dethrone Maxwell Serpente. You see, a couple years back, before I was transferred to work for Serpente, I met with the leader of the Guardians Russia branch. He went on this entire bout of rhetoric trying to convince me of the corruption inside the Serpent Corps. It wasn't until I began to work here that I realized… he was right. Maxwell Serpente may have built this organization from the ground up, and I wouldn't dream of giving up on it, but it is time for him to step down. The only way that can happen though, is by his own death. Naturally I couldn't be the one to do it. no, I needed someone else. A person over all the Guardians. A paragon. If it wasn't you though, I would move on to the next of your companions. But you, you are stronger than anyone I've seen. Not only did you recover from the destruction of your axes, but you managed to best me in a duel. As far as my judgement goes, you can face the paragon of the Serpent Corps, and win. It is for that reason, that all of you may pass." He moved parallel to the wall and gestured for us to leave. I looked back to see everyone, especially Ryder nodding their heads, so we began to walk past. "However, my cover must not be blown, not even after Serpente is dead. Good luck, and I hope that you succeed, but don't think this means I'll go easy the next we meet."

Once Xavier had finished his soliloquy, he let us pass. It almost felt empowering knowing that not just the Guardians wanted Serpente to be defeated. On top of that... it was someone on the front line. Nevertheless, we slowly made our way through the labyrinth of Ferals and finally infiltrated the Serpent Corps mansion.

"Is it just me or was that surprisingly simple?" Jack asked to everyone once we entered the calescent light of the hallways.

Ruby was the first to answer his question as walked through the main halls. "Exactly, the first part is always the easy part. It only gets harder from here, after all, we still have to make our way through the inner sanctum of the fortress. In other words, Serpente's office."

The walls themselves were as drab as I remembered. Still made of the same gray cinderblocks, only parting for the doorways leading to the research rooms for Serpente's overly sadistic projects.

It was Jack who soon took the helm, walking us through the halls, acting almost like a tour guide. In the meantime, he told us about the other Serpent Corps members.

"Talia and I were sparring partners in my days here. It seemed strange thinking about it now but, with all the time we spent together, we became good friends with each other. It's funny how kids fight with such innocence, as if they don't even know what they're fighting for. They just make the best of it, but to someone who doesn't understand this, it's creepy, almost sadistic. She acted like this all the time, and I saw her raw potential. It's quite ironic though, now I realize what I was training her to do."

At some point I noticed we were walking past a sign marked botanical gardens, and upon closer look, I noticed a couple vines protruding out of the cement.

Jack continued being oblivious to where he was heading, as if the rout to Serpente's office was imprinted in his mind. "I never talked much to Hunter or Xavier, but I do know that they were always working together on the field. They were like mentors for each other, and even now they seem to be close friends."

We walked into the botanical gardens, filled to the brim with a veritable supply of plant life. "I think there was one other too, recruited about a year after I left. In fact, I only know about her existence because Joel told me about her. A young girl, but he didn't get the chance to tell of her power, or even her name."

As he spoke, I felt a small tickle at my ankle. I stopped and looked down to see that a vine had wrapped itself around one of my legs. I pulled back in fear alerting the others of the intruder's attack.

"Pwah ha ha." I immediately heard someone burst out in laughter, but nobody was present. "Oh my God! That never gets old, and it doesn't even stop there." The sound had come from behind one of the tables where a very young girl walked out to face us. "Go ahead, look at the rest of your feet." I looked ahead of me at everyone else to see the same vines wrapped tightly around their legs. "My own handy work. It's actually a little sad that Master Serpente won't allow me to enter the field till I turn twelve. Well, I guess this can last me four years."

Immediately the vines tightened on my legs, cementing them in place, allowing only the movement of my arms. I had only one thing to say though. "What are you?"

The girl once again giggled, her forest green skirt ruffling in the process. "I knew that you would ask that first, and I'll allow it for the moment."

Her very long, black hair, pulled back into a ponytail swayed from side to side as she spoke. "I am the wielder of plants as my weapon. The youngest and in my opinion, strongest of all the disciples to Maxwell Serpente. Ivy Storm. Codename, the Power Botanist."

"So, your power is to grow plants?" Jack snorted. In reality it was quite impressive. The vines Ivy used to constrain us all to the ground pulled so hard that none of us were able to move.

Ivy shrugged her shoulders, not picking up on Jack's verbal attack. "You could say that. My power includes growing, shrinking, moving, essentially all control over plant life. but I digress." She paused as if waiting for us to interrupt.

"Do you even know what that means?" Cinder retorted. I wondered how long it would take for Ivy to get bored and decide to end us.

Ivy once again shrugged her shoulder. "I hear it from miss Morris all the time. I think I used it right, but you must feel silly being trapped by an eight-year-old. I thought Talia would at least do in one of you, and then Xavier would finish off what's left. I should have known they would both fail. It looks like it's up to me now. But which one do I get rid of first?"

"Well then," Jack began to retort. "What ever happened to sugar and spice?"

Ivy once again scowled, a fire sparking in her eye. I felt the vines around my leg tighten even more, nearly cutting off circulation. "Shut your mouth traitor. I can snap your legs in half like a stick of celery if I wanted to. After all, it doesn't matter how I kill you. In fact, I might even be celebrated for being so ruthless."

I felt the pressure on my legs release slightly as my legs were hoisted above my head. I immediately saw that the same had happened to my other four companions.

Another set of vines began to wrap around my core, tightening with every new layer, restraining my arms. I turned and looked straight at me. "I really am sorry about the second set kid, but I can't have you breaking my babies with those axes of yours." She said, calming her face, but adding fuel to her inner-fire. "Now let me see, how did that nursery rhyme go again? Sugar and spice and everything nice. That's what little girls are made of. For as long as I remember, my mother said this to me every night before I would go to sleep. She was always full of love and ready to give to whoever needed it. She believed the best for me. She wished for me to have a life full of sugar, spice, and everything nice. My father though, he did not want this to happen."

I felt every vine around me tighten as she told her story. Anger welled up with every word she spoke. "Every night I was forced to listen to his constant abuse of her. Every slap, every name, every cry for help was complete agony. Do you know what it's like to be forced to watch someone being hurt by another and know that you will never be able to help? That man took everything from me."

A small stream of tears fell from her face while she spoke, continuing to wrap vines around my legs. "Then, one night… it was too much for her. She yelled back, wanting to leave him and in return, his anger overflowed… and he pushed he to the ground. That's when the kicking started… continuing until all the life was taken from her, right in front of my eyes." The tears on her face continued to fall at an even more rapid rate. "I was six at the time. I was so innocent. After all the years I still believed that he was a good man, but then I realized, there was never any good in him from the very start. All he did was steal away other people's happiness. Replacing it with his own hateful rage and pain."

A small grin fell on Ivy's face, but the tears continued to fall. "That was the end of it. with these very vines, these very powers granted to me to make things right. He never hurt anyone after her. There was nothing left of him."

Everyone's mouth began to fall at her words. She could have simply restrained and turned her father into the police for murder, but instead she committed full blown patricide. A crime that should never be committed, even if it was to avenge the murder of her

194

mother. Plus, all of this happened when she was only six. What child would do such a thing. I was normally prone to resenting all my mother's old boyfriends, but I would never intentionally harm them, no matter how much of a deadbeat they were.

Ivy continued again, leaving the rest of us speechless. "But that's the entire world isn't it? Just a bunch of leeches waiting to take away your entire life. After all, the only reason people exist in this day and age is to lie and cheat their way to the top, only to take everything that's left, leaving nothing-."

"That's enough!" Ryder yelled, cutting off the young girl's monologue.

Ivy winced at the sudden response. The stream of tears had stopped their flow, leaving imprints on her cheeks, but I could tell she was still holding back. She seemed as if she was ready to end our lives at any moment. "You know that I'm right. After all, why else are you trying to kill my master. He is the exact same person."

"So why don't you just leave him?" Cinder asked while straining under the pressure of the vines. "Why do you choose to work with him if you know he's everything you despise?"

Ivy's answer was short and very unexpected. "In order to catch a snake, you need a snake. All that's left is your deaths and I can finally begin to fix this world."

As she finished speaking, I felt the vines begin to constrict, wrapping themselves whenever they could. The only thing I could hear was Ivy's cynical voice. "You know, originally I wanted to use poisoned oak, but I found it to be way too crazy even for me. So instead, I chose to use good old wisteria." The pressure continued to build as my circulation was slowly cut off.

"I have no other choice," I barely heard Jack say. What followed next was unexpected as sparks began to form between his fingers one more.

"Never... let... go." The words left his mouth, purging all the darkness in our hearts. A ball of electricity larger than I had ever seen before began to expand from his palm, out of his hand, angled towards the vines at his waist. The ball continued to spark and grow until it reached the desired size. Jack then released his fingers leaving only the ball of static, and then... the ball ruptured and exploded into a beam which shattered the vines that were binding him.

Jack fell to the ground, standing to his feet, while Ivy stood in shock. "They may be strong, but even your vines aren't indestructible."

Ivy scowled trying to fathom the sudden explosion. "No, that's not fair. That's impossible. How could you free yourself from my binds? Not even the strongest of men can do that."

Jack struck a confident smile and replied earnestly. "My past is dark, but it gives me strength." Another ball of static began to form in the palm of his other hand. "You're wrong about everything. Human kind is not meant to steal and cheat, we are here to heal. You would know that if you would look outside of the Serpent Corps." The static ball once again began to rupture as Jack aimed his hand at Ivy... and released his fingers. In a gigantic flash of light, the ball of electricity exploded, breaking the vines that banded everyone else, and knocking Ivy unconscious.

The first thing I noticed when my blood wasn't rushing to my head was Jack's hand. He had detonated a blast in each hand, leaving both of them scarred and bloodied.

I was once again stunned. "Jack, what the heck was that?" I asked, standing up from the pile of bramble.

Jack turned away from Ivy's body to face all of us, a solemn look on his face. "Never let go, My ultimate attack. Electricity courses through my body and gathers in my hands. The power continues to grow, taking over all objects in the area, and sucking in everything that is attacked, before exploding once more. I also can use it as a beam attack which I've known to break through solid steel. In return though, my hands are forced into the blast and can take serious damage. The more power I use, the more physical damage my body takes." Everyone stayed silent as Jack caught his breath. "I guess you could even say that the power stems from my memories of the Serpent Corps. The first time I used it was when I escaped a couple years back."

"Shooting lasers from your fingers. Ironic," I said with a small chuckle. The power itself held multiple capabilities, all of them focusing on Jacks strength of will. Then, my focus shifted to the little girl lying unconscious on the floor. "Is she going to be okay?"

Jack walked back to the defenseless girl, and graciously picked her up in both arms. "She'll be fine. Though she probably won't wake up for a couple hours, but then she'll be back to her normal, psychotic self."

Once Ivy was set down on one of the garden ledges, Ruby pulled out a small roll of bandages from her pocket. "Here, let me fix your hands."

Jack refused though by holding up a hand full of gashes which were already beginning to clot. "My wounds will heal. It's best not to waste the time."

Ruby shrugged. "Suit yourself," She said while putting the roll back into her pocket.

Jack looked down at the piles of bramble laying on the floor, and then back at the girl lying lifelessly next to him. "Unless there are any more surprises, the last of Serpente's disciples is Hunter," he said trying to regain his balance.

"Is that a problem?" Ruby began to ask, pondering on the target at hand.

"Isn't it obvious?" Jack walked to the exit of the room, losing balance with each step until he finally grasped the wall. "He's the last stand until we get to Serpente's study. He would obviously station his strongest asset where he needs him most."

"Or he want's Hunter to think he's the best so that he fights harder," I added.

"The kid's pride is his weakness. No matter how good he thinks he is, the bloodlust he keeps can be his undoing," Ryder said while following Jack."

"Either way, he will fight the hardest. Whether it's out of pride or want to protect his master." Jack finished, leading everyone out of the botanical gardens, and towards our last opponent.

The opposite hallway from the botanical gardens was the exact opposite of the entrance. While the hallway we entered from was dimly lit and plain, this hallway was very decorated, to the point where there was even wallpaper like an actual house would have. There were even pictures of other members of the Serpent Corps lining some of the walls.

"Huh, seems quite homey," Cinder began to say. "I have to admit, Serpente has quite a touch for interior decoration."

"Strange that he would take the time to decorate to this level of detail, especially since there are only a select few who are allowed to even see the inner sanctum of this... fortress," Ryder said, staring at some of the pictures as if he recognized the people in them. "It's like he wanted this to seem like a real house." He had been strangely quiet this entire time, only speaking a select few times. The reason was obvious though. Who wouldn't be at least the slightest bit uncomfortable about having to kill their original student?

The hallway quickly opened up into a large library. A perfectly circular room, where the walls were filled with shelves stacked full of books, as if there were almost every book ever published. A single person sat in the in the middle of the large arena like room. He sat in a crossed leg, meditative position, his only movement being his hard breathing. Every part of it screamed last stand before the final boss. It was obvious, this boy was the gravity master, Hunter Haines.

A single step into the circular library was all it took to alert him. With a single step forward, his eyes opened and his back straitened. All the bloodlust I had seen the night before was still there, but for some reason, he seemed surprised.

"Would you look at that. It's only been an hour and a half, and you've already gotten through Talia, Xavier, and even Ivy. All of you Guardians are so interesting. I thought it would take at least an hour more."

I took another step out of the hallway, allowing my companions to join me. Hunter rolled his eyes and continued what I assumed to be a hideous aspersion. "Seriously, I thought Ivy would at least waste one of you, or keep you for another hour with her childish rants. But I guess it makes sense. Leave it to me to pick up the slack for everyone else."

"Well someone's self-absorbed," Ruby retorted. "You really expect to kill all of us by yourself?"

Hunter shrugged, smirking in the process. "I might."

"You're insane," Cinder said very cynically.

"Not in the slightest my dear. It isn't that my ego is bigger than I let on or anything. I'm just that powerful." Hunter lifted two of his circular chakram from the hardwood floor. The steel shimmered under the light on the high ceiling. "There is a simple saying for all of this. In every battle, there is the wolf and the cattle. The wolf will become the hunter, and the cattle will become nothing more than the wolf's next meal."

"So... your point?" Cinder asked.

Hunter struck a triumphant pose and once again spoke. "Don't you get it? I am the wolf. I am the hunter, and you are nothing but my pray."

Hunter spun his arms, releasing both of his Chakrams. The circular blades spun at high speed across the room, poised for its target, coming ever closer to Ruby and Cinder who were standing at the far sides of the entrance.

Moving in sequence of each other, both Ruby and Cinder pulled out their weapons to deflect the incoming projectile. Ruby parried the attack with her sword, and Cinder used the metal plating on her bow.

Hunter smirked at the two girls who had deflected the shot. "Not that easy girls," he said while holding out his hand. The chakrams redirected themselves and began to once again reach their targets. Only this time, the girls leapt out of the way, allowing the weapons to fall to the ground and completely stop.

Ruby picked up one of the lifeless objects from the floor, her eyes glossing over in silver the moment her hands clasped the handles. She then proceeded to mimic Hunter's movements with exact precision, only this time, Hunter stepped out of the way, only to once again hold up a hand, causing the blade to spin back towards its owner who willingly caught it in his open hand.

"Got to say, not my style at all," Ruby snorted. "Ranged weapons have never been my favorite."

Hunter once again rolled his eyes. "Well, for someone with my power it works like a charm." Once again, he held out his other hand which caused the other chakram to pull toward him. I couldn't help but notice how he was gazing straight at me, and with another throw, the circular blade began to fly once more. Just as I had done the previous night, I phased two axes and blocked the attack. This time though, to avoid being locked into a corner, I ran out of the blade's trajectory, strait at my attacker.

Once I was within five feet of Hunter, I began the attack, spinning the axe in my hand just as I had seen Xaraxis do less than an hour ago. Only when I was inches from him though did he choose to defend, pulling his other chakram to my axe blade, and punching me in the stomach with his free hand.

"That isn't going to work a second time Ronen, much less on me," Hunter yelled as I fell to the floor. He stood back, both of his weapons now in his hands. "Curtains, you're done." He then proceeded to thrust the blade down in an attempt to end me. only when he was halfway down, he was met by two separate disturbances. The first was an arrow fired at one of Hunter's shoulders, and the second was a shock of static electricity fired from Jack's hand.

Hunter wretched slightly at the duel attack but didn't fall. It was actually pretty impressive considering that one shot from Cinder's arrows was enough to completely knock out Talia. However, the sudden shock allowed me just enough time to escape from his attack.

Despite being a few feet from him, I still couldn't fully escape the range of Jack's attack. My leg went numb, feeling more and more motionless with every step I took.

Returning to the rest of my companions, I noticed Ryder standing stock still. "His power really does outmatch all the other disciples," I heard him say under his breath. Then noticing my presence, he turned to face me. "I have one idea." He pointed about fifty meters past Hunter to the other side of the room. "Serpente's office is right there. The only way I can think of that gives us a chance is if you make a run for it while the others distract Hunter."

"But we can take him down, it's only a matter of time. Besides, what happened to the whole never fight him alone thing?" I said trying to understand the magnitude of what he was saying.

Ryder shook his head. "We don't have the time for that. There isn't another choice. We could even try using ultimate abilities and that may not even confirm our victory. You can still get there though, but it has to be alone."

I immediately denied everything he told me. "No. No I can't do that. I can't do this alone. I won't."

"It's the only way we even have a chance at this Ronen, trust me." He looked straight in my eyes and once again spoke. "Go."

At the same time, I felt another hand on my shoulder. Standing behind me was the trans-mundane spirit who was the embodiment of my own power: Xaraxis. "He's right. This gives us the best chance we have, but remember, you aren't going in alone."

I took a deep breath, and nodded, understanding what I had just been told, and once again looked back to the door leading to Maxwell Serpente's office. The rest could keep Hunter occupied in the time it would take me, there was no question in that. It would give me enough time to run to the door, but it would be my only chance.

In a single moment, I ran to the door without so much as gaining Hunter's attention. I looked back once more my companions each working to keep Hunter at bay and finally opened the door. I looked forward at the open office and entered the final room of the Serpent Corps fortress.

*   *   *   *   *

The first thing I noticed upon entering was the rolling desk chair turned away from me. The only thing that would make it more cliché is if Serpente turned and was stroking a cat, but I dared not laugh. "You know, some part of me always knew it would come down to this," I heard the voice of Serpente saying. "Mono y mono. The strongest of all the Serpent Corps against the only arguably strongest and newest member of the Guardian agents."

"You know how this is going to end Serpente. Give up now and this will come easy," I said with confidence, knowing what answer would come.

"That is what you think, young Ronen." I heard again from Serpente. Then a new voice took over, sounding much more feminine than Serpente could ever be.

"However, … it may seem that you are terribly wrong." The chair began to swivel around, revealing its keeper. It was not Serpente, but a girl with flowing black hair, looking much older than me, wearing black pumps. It was obvious. This was not Serpente, but his assistant, Mickala Morris.

"How did you…? Where is Serpente?"

Mickala smiled wryly and stood from the chair. "He isn't here, nor has he been in nearly two days. Instead, I am here to finish you off."

For the umpteenth time, I shook my head in disbelief. "You and I both know that's impossible though. Even with your time sight, your power sees through every possibility. No matter how you look at it, I outmatch you."

She didn't say anything. Instead, she set down what looked to be a voice recorder and pulled an unknown object out from a desk drawer. "What you say may be true on the surface, but I have found that there is always a surefire way for me to win every time." She raised the object, revealing it to be a black syringe filled with some sort of deep black substance. The same substance that was used on me before. "From what he has told me, Maxwell likes to call it… the Hellsing serum. It possesses multiple capabilities including that of bringing the worst tendencies of a person to the surface. Every bit of anger, abhorrence, and bloodlust are brought out, creating the ultimate berserker. But of course, you're familiar with that now… aren't you."

Based on how she explained it, there was nothing good that came from that drug, as if it was synthesized from the devil's nectar itself. "Mickala, don't do this. You take that... and there's no going back."

Mickala sneered at me with an undying hatred. "Oh... I already know," she said before jamming the needle into her neck and releasing the black liquid into her bloodstream.

Get ready kid. This could get ugly.

Within seconds, her body was engulfed in bloodlust, as muscles begin to form under her skin. Her eyes glossed over in a blue hue, before being engulfed in a black fire. "Now Ronen... there is one thing left for you to do. Die!" Her face was twisted in anger as she shrieked.

I phased a pair of axes, and took a fighting stance, ready for the most difficult fight I would encounter thus far. The fight that would change my life.

13

If it were possible to quantify the amount of energy in a human body, mine would only have around ten percent remaining. That didn't stop me from fighting though. My anxiety from four consecutive fights (the second of which I had released Xaraxis) was almost too much for me to handle. A couple more minutes and overflow would surely happen, but I couldn't give up. Not just yet. Not while I still had one more opponent.

I stared at the body of Mickala Morris, twisted with bloodlust. Though nothing but slight muscle growth had changed in her physical body, her eyes held a scorching inferno hot enough to burn down a national forest. She had screamed out wanting my death, desperate to win, and called upon a greater bloodlust that only actual blood could satisfy. But I had no intention of giving it up.

In a quick motion, she picked up a large, slender staff from the side of the desk. The black, metallic finish reflected off of the overhead lights with ease.

Something about the fact that she would choose to use a bow staff seemed fitting, and also out of place at the same time.

Mickala held the staff across her chest and without saying a single word, pushed forward ready to strike. She only left a fraction of a second for reaction, and instead I was simply left to hold off her attacks by using my axes as a shield, and right as they intersected, Mickala swung her staff into my defense with all her strength. However, in the process she left a window of opportunity for me to attack.

I allowed the axe in my right hand to drop only to simultaneously create another axe which I swung at her exposed ribs. In an instant, my axe grazed her shirt and... she pulled back. To have such speed as to be able to dodge such an attack was purely impossible, but she had done it right before my eyes, and seemed to be much prouder of herself than she should have.

"I totally get it," Mickala began to say almost spitefully. "How can someone like me stand to dodge your kill shot. Well, I'm not about to express how much better I am than you like Mr. Haines would. No, this is something completely different. A sort of Cerebral Study if you'd prefer to think of it that way. I've never had to call out its name or anything like that, but it can sure come in handy once I activate it."

I didn't want to believe it. On top of knowing my exact attacks, it was as if she had read my thoughts as they happened. She could know every attack, every defense, and every strategy I could think of. There was no use arguing it, this was her ultimate ability, but she didn't need to call out a name when she activated it. Her mental capabilities were strong enough that she could trigger that image in an instant. She knew my every move.

"This little revolution ends today! As will you Ronen Haven!" Mickala yelled as she brandished her staff again, ready to charge. I had no ability to use, no matter what I did she would know my strategy. But I still couldn't give up. I couldn't allow her to kill me. I knew if I did, every hope for defeating Serpente would be lost.

I continued to use the same tactic of shield and counter I had used before, allowing her to attack once more, and again, and again, until finally, the green axes chipped and finally shattered, leaving me completely defenseless. By the time the shards hit the ground, Mickala had connected another attack, hitting me to the ground.

"Huh, funny, I always thought this would be harder, but yet you fall so easy. Perhaps using the Hellsing serum was unnecessary after all." She paused, holding the staff to her side. "No big deal. Maxwell doesn't care how hard it is to kill you, just that it gets done."

Her power was unmatched. Something I should have expected from Serpente's assistant. She had drained everything from me. There was no fight left. I had no other choice but to accept my fate and allow myself to give up control to the one force that could stand a chance. I closed my eyes... and waited, only for nothing to happen. I was still stuck on the floor, unable to fight.

Mickala Morris continued to gloat, getting louder as she chided me. "You know, I'm actually quite disappointed. After all, I never even got to see your fabled transformation, or your... oh what do you Guardians call them, ultimates? Here we just call them final strikes, mostly because they are used to end your enemy, like so."

I didn't hear a word she told me; all I could think of was that I was letting my friends down. They were right outside the door to Serpente's office, fighting for their lives. Giving everything, they had with hopes that I was doing the same. I had let them down. I couldn't even land a single hit.

"You have one choice to make kid, and you know what it is," I heard from inside my head. Xaraxis was still there, and he was right too. There was one thing I could try, but I wanted to avoid it. I didn't want to see what it would do. I didn't want to lock him away again. I just couldn't do that to him.

But out of the blue, the voice once again spoke to me. *"As long as your heart is in the right place, it will work. Trust me kid. I need you for this."*

Under his orders, I reached deep into my pockets and pulled out a small rope... attached to it was a metal cross with six bands. Four were around each of the ends, and the other two overlapped in the middle. In a quick motion, completely devoid of thought, the amulet that was once stolen from me, was thrust over my head.

As the metal hit my chest, a figure appeared before me. black stripes cascaded past his right eye and down his arms into the middle of his hand. His hair the color of mine fell just past his eyes. A figure of darkness, anger, but understanding. He reached out his hand. Hoping for true understanding. Wanting me to join him. "For once, I can give my power to you."

I felt a certain presence of both warmth and understanding. It seemed to swaddle every part of me, and even though I was in the heat of my most dangerous battle. It seemed ironic, but I was completely at peace with myself.

I looked up at him, ignoring the fact that Serpente's executioner was standing over me. "I thought you said it was impossible."

"With the normal power, maybe. But there is always more," he began to say as he held his hand to my shoulder. "Ronen… It's time."

With those words, I knew that what he was saying was true. I tightly clasp my hand to his. "We can do this… together," I said, reassuring both of us.

As soon as the words left my lips, two flames burst forth from both of us just as it had before, the green and black flames spired together, enveloping the two of us in both green and black flames. There was no fear, no anxiety, and no anger. All of it left my body at once, burned up by the flames, and Xaraxis fused with my own self till we were one with each other. The same mind. The same body. The same person.

I screamed out the first thing that came to mind. "This is true control." It was a voice that could lead a revolution. Both of us finally working together on the same plane. I felt my power multiply by an infinite amount with every second, giving me a will to fight.

Mickala Morris seemed pleased, but still had the edge of hatred given to her by the Hellsing serum. "Finally. Now it's time for the real fight to start."

I created yet another set of axes, ready to strike their targets. Only both axes were not the color I was used to. They were both swirled in the colors black and green. "This ends now. It's time for you to die Miss Morris."

The woman before me snarled with confidence. "I'd love to see you try to make that happen."

What followed was a barrage of swings, both from Mickala Morris and the hybrid of both Xaraxis and I. Neither side let up. Only now, our attacks could overpower her staff. All of my anxiety was taken, and in its place was strength and confidence. This was what happened all along. The stress my body took only strengthened my transformation. Throughout the days I knew him, Xaraxis knew this, and he was nothing but understanding.

This was the true meaning behind my power. This was what control embodied. A power that took every negative emotion and turned it into strength. The part of me that had to die to make something beautiful.

Mickala Morris snarled with anger, beginning to become unglued. "I will not be defeated by some wretch half my age! I will not! I will not!"

Her bloodlust was all that could be seen anymore. All the composure I had seen before was gone, leaving only anger, envy, and grief. From inside both our minds, I heard Xaraxis speak. "She's slipping kid. Let's end this."

Without responding, I knew everything he wanted from me. In a single second I executed the attack. I spun my body and thrusted one of my axes forward. I spun full rotation and planted my axes right inside Mickala Morris's ribcage.

Immediately, she fell on the ground, ready to be vanquished. I stood above her, my axes above my head ready to swing before…

"Wait, there's something you need to know."

The voice came from Mickala Morris lying flat on the ground. Her voice was once again calm and composed. All her bloodlust had dissipated. I looked down, my eyes locking onto hers. "What?"

Once again in her composed mid-pitch voice, Mickala spoke. "I want… I want… to thank you… for freeing me."

I fell down on one knee at her words, unable to speak as she continued. "Years ago, I worked under Serpente as one of his interns. Out of the other three competitors, I won, but I didn't realize what would come from it. I was forced to watch the fates of the losers, absorbed by Serpente's power as a form of incentive not to mess up. And just like that my new job… no, my new life started. I was his creation. His art. He filled me with his own hatred and bloodlust until I finally turned into the quiet monster you saw. I learned to forget my past, believing that I had spent my entire life here, with him.

I didn't understand what she was saying. "How did you know?"

Mickala Morris coughed loudly, spitting up drops of blood in the process. "I've always known something was wrong, and every clue slowly untied the knot. It was all to an end. Every secret was nothing but a trick. I didn't remember my past, or how I even got here, but I knew I was still asleep. His hatred continued to leech off of me and I soon forgot why I was even looking for clues in the first place. I forgot everything, but I always knew about Serpente's evil. It wasn't until just now that you snapped me out of it. I remember everything, I just wish my death didn't have to come with it."

She spoke with a very noticeable rasp and I couldn't understand some of what she said, but I knew she was close to death. The place where I had wounded her was slowly filling with crimson fluid. Within a couple minutes, she would bleed out.

I looked into her hazy eyes, still seeing life in them. "I can help you. One of my friends has bandages. If I hurry, you'll be alright."

Mickala shook her head, a sensitive smile on her face. "I'm afraid that's not possible. The wound is just too deep. Don't worry about me though. I am at peace with it. I have been for a long time."

I was no longer resonating with Xaraxis and had to believe that my ability had worn off. I felt a wave of sudden weakness wash over me, but Mickala continued to speak.

"Listen closely Ronen, because I don't have much time. Over the years I have seen through thousands of possible futures. Possibilities you couldn't even think of. Possibilities where you never become a Guardian or die trying to attack this facility. There's even one where you fight with us on the Serpent

Corps. But out of every possibility that I've watched past this point, Serpente dies in only three. My weakness prevents me from showing you the full future, but I can leave some bread crumbs."

Mickala slowly crept her hand to touch my chest, right where my heart was. She then uttered another set of words.

"Life release… Spear of time."

Once those words left her lips, my mind went blank. In its place were three visions. The first was of a picture of five people posed in front of a pyramid. I immediately recognized the person on the far left. Every morning I would wake up and see him in the mirror. Beside me were the other four Guardians: Ruby, Jack, Cinder, and Ryder.

The picture soon changed to that of what seemed to be an Arabian bazaar during rush hour. Every stand marked with signs of another language were packed to the point where I was unable to register anyone's face.

The scene once again distorted to a third image. An image of Maxwell Serpente in a dark background, running away, a look of sheer terror plastered on his face. Behind him was a bolt of what looked to be dark-violet colored lightning. It was very distinct and seemed to be the attack he was running from.

As the third image faded away, I once again saw the inside of Serpente's office. Mickala Morris still laid on the floor bleeding out. I looked at her eyes to see them begin to lose all feeling. Along with her death, she said one last thing.

"I have shown you these visions so that you will know what to do when the time comes. Serpente will never see it coming, and his defeat will finally happen. I trust you Ronen... trust you to overcome this world. I wish you the best of luck."

I watched as her breath slowed to a crawl, and then halted for good. Mickala Morris, The Serpent Corps scryer, was dead. With a flat palm, I closed her eyes and stood up once more. "Thank you miss Morris. I will not let you down."

I turned back to the study door to see it open again. Without any kind of hesitation, Ruby walked in with a face of half remorse and half joy, probably thinking Serpente had been defeated. She looked right at me, then at the body of Mickala Morris. Then, with eyes about to pop out of her skull, she finally said something. "What just happened in here?"

I looked back in remorse. "Serpente isn't here," I told her, wishing for it to be a lie. "He never was."

*　　　*　　　*　　　*　　　*

In surprise of their eventual victory over Hunter Haines, I told them everything that had happened with Mickala Morris. Including her final move. Like I expected, they couldn't remove their look of shock.

Ruby seemed the least surprised out of all of them. "Life release," she began to say as I finished my recap. "The forbidden move. What could cause her to use it?"

"What exactly is it?" I asked.

Ruby looked away from all of us before answering. "It's the most powerful move that comes with the Guardian gene. It can grant a single wish

216

greater than any power possible, but as payment, ends the life of the user. It does have to follow the core rules of the Guardians though, so it won't result in hypnosis or anything.

Ryder took over for her once she finished her description. "So, she told you how to kill Serpente?"

I shook my head. "No, not exactly. It's more like… she showed me parts of it, if I follow the right path." I looked back down at the lifeless body of Mickala Morris. The gash I had made in her ribcage had stopped leaking, having drained her body entirely. But there was one thing I noticed. One thing I hadn't seen before. I reached down to her hand and pulled a small sky-blue ring off her finger. I examined it closely to see what looked to be the face of an owl on it. I looked back to everyone, holding the ring in my hand. "Hey, what is this?"

Ryder came up to me with a face of utter amazement. "Could it be? Did we actually find one of them?"

"One of what?"

Ryder held up the ring to his eye, inspecting it. "One of the Rings of Isis. Another artifact."

Everyone stared back in amazement of the mysterious item. Clearly it was incredibly important to them. "And that is-?" I began to say, until Ryder instantly answered her.

"Isis of Giza was one of the original Guardians. She could teleport anything to or away from herself at will. Her artifact was a ring which granted her clarity. She could see the status of all people, including if a Guardian has activated one of their

217

abilities or not. When the Serpent Corps uncovered it, they smelted the ring down, and crafted seven separate rings, each having the ability to see a different aspect of human life. Serpente gave each one to the closest and most trusted of agents, all over the globe. It seems that this one did in fact give her the ability to see if a Guardian had activated an ability. Which means-"

I cut him off to finish what he was saying in shock. "She knew. She wanted me to be stronger because she knew I needed this power to defeat Serpente, even if it meant her death." I began to wish that she was on our side, a perfect asset and friend to have.

The sudden realization brought everyone to shock, but that didn't stop Ryder. He clearly seemed surprised at the actions of Mickala Morris, but there was more. He was looking forward.

"This experience has been completely surprising. I'm sure the rest of the Guardian council will be very interested to hear of these events. I'll have to notify them at the next world council meeting. This will certainly change everything."

"Shouldn't we alert someone higher up first. Like, I don't know the leader of the United States branch?" I asked, ready to lower my jaw at whatever he was about to tell me.

"We won't have a need to worry ourselves with such a thing," Ryder began. "You are looking at him after all."

Just as I had anticipated, Ryder had shocked me. "You're kidding?" I asked skeptically, only to get a simple nod in return.

I almost threw my hands up into the air out of surprise. "And when were you planning on telling me this exactly?"

Ryder shrugged. "The flow of information that was supposed to take place in your training was a short stream. I would have explained it eventually. That much is true."

At that point I didn't even have the chance to sigh, after all I knew very well that there was a veritable mine filled with information, I had no idea existed.

From then on, everyone stayed silent, except for Jack who stayed calm the entire time, and slowly picked up his head. "Well... there's no use sulking over the complete one eighty. After all, there is still reason to celebrate."

"Like what?" I asked him, very skeptically.

Jack smirked at my oblivious comment. "Isn't it obvious. You unlocked your ultimate ability. Now there is only one more step."

"What?" I asked, still slightly timid

"Name it."

"What?"

"You heard me, give it a name. That way you can call upon it whenever you need to."

I began to ponder on what I could call my newly acquired ability. When I first activated it, I called it true control, but that it was more than just that. The power didn't give me control over Xaraxis. The power brought two parts together, normally separated by reality. There was really one name that came to mind.

"Ultimate authority."

"Nice," Cinder said boldly. "Sounds fitting, and creative."

With nothing left to say, everyone began to leave the room, but something still remained for me to ask. "Hey… Ryder?"

The eldest and yet still young adult looking man turned in the doorway. "Yes?" his face still seemed mysterious, hiding so many secrets from me.

With a single sigh, I told him what I was thinking. "Before… back when I had just joined and all, you told me that the Guardian gene was passed down by a person's parent. Well, what about me?

Ryder walked close and placed a hand on his shoulder. "I knew you would ask that eventually, and I can tell you, if you really want to know."

"Tell me."

Ryder nodded and spoke very slowly. "His name was Cyrus Haven. Your father was part of the California branch. He was a man of many talents that came along with his power, a couple of which he even used to seduce your mother. He was a very bold man, and before he died, he could never stop talking about his son. He couldn't wait to see what you would turn into."

I couldn't help but smile. My mother had always avoided talking about my father, and I had never even heard his name. Probably because my mother had lost the best thing to ever happen to her. "What was his power?"

Ryder smirked, remembering my father. "Accuracy. The power came from his sense of balance in mind, body and soul. When you put a weapon of long range in his hand, he could hit a target from half a mile away. The perfect assassin. That being said, I never met a man with such a love for life."

"That's nice. I'm glad to hear it. He sounds like a good guy."

"He was. He was a good man," Ryder said, still reminiscing. "I guess at this point, we have no choice but to go home, lick our wounds, and prepare for what is to come."

I nodded to his comment, ready to conclude the mission that was never completed. "You're right. But... there's one more thing that should be added to that list."

14

The crisp winter air brushed across my thin jacket, leading to my bare skin. It had seemed like ages ago when I first left. Time acted differently in my training, and a part of me just didn't want it to end. But another part of me longed to feel a certain warmth again. A warmth I had kept close to me for my entire life but had gone without for nearly three weeks. It hadn't been that long, but in that short of time I knew I had changed more than in my entire life.

A warm hand was placed on my shoulder. A hand belonging to a now close friend who had taught me more about myself than anyone else. The hand of Ryder, my mentor. On either side of us stood Ruby to my immediate right, and Cinder along with Jack on either end. They had been my teachers, aiding me in my journey. A journey that couldn't have been over.

I couldn't help but stare forward at the townhouse I was raised in. my mother was poised inside, waiting for me to return to her once more. "I can't believe I'm about to do this. After all this time," I said still in thought.

"Don't think too much into it. You deserve this," Ruby assured me while also cutting me off. "You may not have defeated Serpente, but you've certainly bought us some time."

Ryder nodded in unison with everyone else. "With the defeat of Mickala Morris we not only have crippled the infrastructure of the Serpent Corps, but we have clues on how to finally destroy Serpente. In time, he will be defeated."

I continued to ponder over the three visions shown to me by Mickala Morris. The last one in particular. Serpente was running away. No... he was being chased by whoever was shooting the violet lightning. Obviously, this was not one of my powers, nor could it have been me using the life release ability. That could have only meant...

"I'm not the one who defeats Serpente. I'm not the one from the prophecy"

Ryder shook his head as if he knew more than I did. "Remember what I said. The easiest way to vitiate Serpente's power is by using a partner. I wouldn't say you're out of the picture just yet."

"For now, though, it's time for you to return home," Cinder said while ushering me out of the tree line towards my own house. I could also hear Ruby speak to me as I left them.

"We'll keep in touch to continue your training."

I walked towards the house, remembering all that I had gone through in only a matter of three weeks. Every task completed, every battle won, and every battle lost and taken as strength. I had learned more about who I was in this time than I had in my entire life, and I had them all to thank for it, but I had still only grasped the surface.

So, I ask again Ronen, what is it exactly that you truly want?

I could hear Xaraxis entirely clear, and his words couldn't have been better chosen. Over just three weeks I had actually begun to feel happy. I had begun to feel like I belonged to something. I had unlocked a part of myself which always felt like it was missing.

"I don't think I need to answer that question. I already have what I always needed." I said under my breath while looking back at the rest of the Guardians huddled together.

Immediately, a multitude of memories since I had become a Guardian came flooding into my mind:

The long mornings and nights I spent training with Ruby. She had done her best to imbue all her knowledge into me, and she had succeeded. If it weren't for her, I would have never been able to face anyone, let alone myself.

When Jack rescued me from the Serpent Corps after I was drugged. It was his protection, his knowledge, and his past which had given us the information we needed to prevail in the end.

The moment I shared a dance with Cinder the night before the siege, where she had pretty much revealed her entire soul to me. Because of her I was finally able to realize the power that had been hidden in my own trauma and connect with my other form.

And the moment in that forest when Ryder had found me. I was scared and irrational at the time. But in the end, he rescued me. He brought me to a new understanding of myself, and introduced me to a new family.

They had all given me what I needed in their own special ways, and I owed everything to the group I was now the fifth member of.

I turned around before finally returning home. "Jack, Ruby, Ryder, Cinder. Thank you. For... everything." Each one of them were smiling, all of them proud of me.

"And after everything, I still have to face her. Mom's so going to kill me." I laughed as I turned back to the house, and grasped the doorknob, ready to finally return home.

With a single movement, I opened the door and entered the small townhouse. The inside was just as I had remembered. The living room was painted the same cream color that my mom adored. Random jackets and sweaters were strewn around the room, as if no one had cleaned since I left.

I saw that the light in the kitchen was on. I knew my mother was there. Quietly, I closed the door and walked to the light, avoiding each place I knew had loose floorboards.

As soon as I was at the doorway, I called out. "Hello... I'm home." It was the same thing I said every day when I got home from school.

I could hear how surprised my mother was. She suddenly dropped one of the ceramic plates she was cleaning on the floor. Only she didn't seem to care about the shattered dining ware. She immediately pulled off her yellow rubber gloves and ran to me. It was the fastest I had ever seen her run.

She wrapped her overly soft hands around me. The tears welling up in her eyes were ready to overflow at any second. She stayed silent, continuing to embrace me with all her strength, only breaking the silence to gasp for air.

I gazed past my mother to see my true companion Xaraxis leaning against the doorframe. This time though, he was smiling. It wasn't pity or condescension, but pride. For the first time, we were both thinking the same thing. "You've done a good job kid." I knew it as much as anyone else. I was finally home.

In time, I learned that my mother did in fact break up with Jerry shortly after my leaving. And with the death of Mickala Morris, Serpente was forced to flee. While the rest of his branches would have to be taken one by one, the main body of the reticulation was destroyed. We had crippled the infrastructure of the organization beyond fixing. In truth, it was Serpente's flight of the scene that was the downfall of the Serpent Corps. Now, the only ones left in the fight were his disciples: Talia, Xavier, Ivy, and Hunter.

There was no telling when their leader, Maxwell Serpente, would resurface to strike again, only to be hunted by the five of us once more. He had nowhere to run and was out of places to hide.

There was one last thing I could say with absolute certainty. When that day finally came… I would be ready.

Made in the USA
Monee, IL
13 March 2020

23105277R00134